THE MOONSTONE CHRONICLES - BOOK FOUR

SARA C ROETHLE

CHAPTER ONE

Saida

Saida stared into the light of the oil lamp. The flickering flames casting shadows on the inside of her tent made her think of Elmerah. Perhaps she would finally be reunited with her friend . . . if the curse she would soon cast didn't kill her.

Brosod felt she would be fine. If she could control the Crown of Cindra, she could handle one measly location curse. But what if she failed? The last time she was cursed, she nearly died. She remembered being trapped in that dark place all too well.

"Saida?" Brosod's voice came from outside the tent. "It's time, the moon is high." She spoke the common tongue near perfectly, though her words held the accent of the Makali and Lukali deep in the Helshone.

Saida stood, glancing around the interior of the small space, hoping for something to delay her, but there was nothing. Just her sleeping mat, a water skin, and the lone lamp. She had a small bundle of other supplies, gifted to her by the Makali clans who'd sworn allegiance to her cause, but little else.

"I'll be right out," she called back, pulling her long white-blonde hair into a quick braid. As much as her instincts were screaming, she shouldn't be delaying, there wasn't much time to spare.

Two weeks. They had less than two weeks to find Elmerah and kill the emperor. If they could not defeat Egrin Dinoba, he would eliminate everyone left in Faerune, including her father. The only other option was for her to turn on Malon and give Egrin the circlets before the full moon.

"Saida?" Brosod asked again, pushing aside the tent flap.

Saida wrung her hands, looking at her friend. Her dark brown skin glowed gold in the lantern light. The curse to locate Elmerah wouldn't have been so frightening if it were to be performed in privacy, but they had an army now. An army of Makali warriors who had provided them with food and shelter across the Helshone. They would make it out of the desert the next morning and head straight for Fallshire for news, and to re-supply. Hopefully by then they would know their following step. They would know where to find Elmerah.

Brosod stepped inside the tent, then leaned on her spear, draping her tan robes around her long legs. "All will be well. It is a simple curse and we have all of the ingredients. It won't be anything like what Urali did to you. And Malon will be there."

She let out a weak laugh. "You say that like his presence is supposed to be comforting. You do know he kidnapped me and threw me into this mess to begin with."

Brosod gave her an indulgent smile, like a patient mother. "Your relationship is complicated, but he makes you feel safe. I can see it. His presence at the ritual will be a comfort to you."

Saida glared at her. "Are Makali always so blunt?"

Brosod grinned, fully revealing her sharp lower canines. "Surviving the Helshone leaves little time for cheap lies. Now we must begin while the moon is at its apex."

"You're sure only having a half-moon tonight won't make things go awry?"

Brosod stepped back toward the tent flap, holding it open for Saida to exit. "Full moon is better, but any moon will do."

She didn't see Malon outside, but she could feel him approaching and knew she could delay no longer. She could sense the Crown of Arcale upon his brow, just as she could feel the gentle magic thrumming from the circlet at her belt. Thinking of it, she untied the cord securing it and settled the circlet atop her head. The moment she did, the strange whispers ensued, oddly soothing. She had heard them many times now. Sometimes they spoke clearly, but mostly it was like being in a room with multiple conversations occurring at once. It could be dizzying, but they made her feel like she wasn't alone.

Brosod stepped out of the tent, still holding the flap open wide.

Saida lifted her nose and walked out into the cool night air, though not as cold as the nights they had spent deep in the Helshone. She still didn't understand how the scorching desert could be colder at night than the more moderate lands just north of it, but she felt silly asking anyone. Perhaps one of the scholars in Faerune could explain it to her, if they survived.

Brosod let the tent flap fall shut behind her, then the two women walked together across the rapidly cooling sand, their loose tan clothing fluttering in the breeze. Neither wore their head wraps. Brosod's close-cropped black hair was bare to the moon overhead.

"I'm scared," Saida admitted, her voice a low murmur.

Brosod didn't have a chance to answer as Malon met them halfway to the distant fires, having come from the direction of his own tent. He wore the same loose tan robes as everyone else. Saida had become so used to the clothing of the Helshone, she knew it would be jarring when she finally saw Malon in northern attire. She wondered what style of dress he would prefer, since he would never again wear the uniform of a guardsmen.

She realized she was staring, and quickly resumed her pace.

Malon fell into step at her side, opposite Brosod. He leaned in near her shoulder, draping his loose silver hair across her arm. "Are you sure about this?"

No, she thought. *No, I'm not sure.* "We must find Elmerah. With her, Isara, and the circlets, our victory against Egrin will be guaranteed."

He spoke no further as they neared the fires set up by the other Makali. The ritual would take place at the largest central fire, its blaze casting glittering light across the yellow sand. Countless Makali watched on as she, Malon, and Brosod stopped before the flames.

Brosod lifted the basket of ingredients she had gathered, then turned toward Saida. "Tonight, you cast your first curse. Tonight, you become a wise woman of our clan."

Saida shivered.

As if sensing the small movement, Malon placed a hand on her shoulder. "I will be here to pull you back if you get lost."

Lost. She could get lost. But if she managed to walk the dream world correctly, she could locate Elmerah. She could save her people. It was a risk she was willing to take.

She reached out a hand toward Brosod. "Let us begin."

Elmerah

The ship gently swayed on the calm sea, futilely attempting to lull Elmerah back to sleep. Judging by the soft breathing coming from the others within the cabin, she was the last one left awake. The lantern overhead slowly swung back-and-forth, casting strange shadows across the other sleeping forms atop their mats. She wiped a bead of sweat from her brow. She had drifted off for about three heartbeats, but the nightmares quickly jolted her back to awareness.

She moved her bandaged hand from her forehead to hold it in front of her face. Even with Vail's healing salve, the burns would leave scars. But the worst effects of what she'd done were buried deep inside her. They only showed themselves on the inside of her eyelids at night, when she would see the countless Dreilore she'd killed in one searing wave of flame. Flame so powerful it had almost burned her alive. She never wanted to touch such power again, but she knew she wouldn't have a choice. Not when a demon emperor was trying to capture her.

Giving up on sleep, she rose from her mat and crept

toward the cabin door. She wasn't sure whose turn it was to man the deck at this time of night, but she would at least find some allies awake beneath the moon above. Moonlight sounded nice. Moonlight and fresh sea air. That's all she needed, then she would be able to rest. *Surely* she would be able to rest. Only two more nights had passed since they'd fled Port Aeluvaria, but those two nights riddled with nightmares weighed heavily upon her.

She grabbed her boots and borrowed brown wool coat on her way out, her old coat having been singed beyond repair. She shut the cabin door gently behind her, then donned the coat and boots in the near darkness. She listened for anyone possibly awake in the neighboring cabins, shook her head, then moved toward the ladder leading up on deck.

The first breath of sea air had her feeling anxious rather than calm, the feeling only multiplied by heavy fog obscuring the moon and stars. She searched the quiet deck for anyone she would care to talk to. She passed over Vessa manning the sails with another nameless elf, and next absolutely dismissed the possibility of conversing with Zirin, the only other Arthali on board besides her and Rissine. He was being followed and clearly pestered by Killian regardless.

Her shoulders relaxed as she finally spotted Alluin heading toward the cabins. He wore a green cloak over his tunic and breeches, the hem fluttering near his knees. He looked utterly out of place on the ship. He belonged in the forest, hunting deer in the sunlight and bathing in streams.

He hesitated for a moment upon noticing her, then closed the distance between them. The lids of his green eyes were heavy, his long brown hair tied back to keep the sea breeze from toying with it. "Why are you awake? You should be resting."

She shrugged. "Couldn't sleep." She wasn't sure what else to say. She wanted to share her nightmares with someone, but Alluin had his own burdens to bear. Still, his nearness brought comfort. He had seen her at her worst, and he hadn't fled. He'd braved death to remain at her side.

He gazed past her toward the open sea. "Something feels strange this night. The fog is unusually thick. Zirin has been unable to clear it with his winds."

She frowned. Even with only a slight breeze to work with, any witch of the Winter Isles clan should be able to clear away the fog. She gestured for Alluin to follow her toward the railing, where they both peered out into the night.

She watched the fog, noticing how it didn't swirl and ebb near the water. There should have been some movement there with the waves choppy from the ship's passing. Gooseflesh erupted on her arms where they weren't still bound tight with bandages beneath her coat. "Something isn't right."

Alluin nodded. "Can you summon a bit of lightning to light up the fog?"

8

Her bandaged hands clenched the railing. She hadn't used her magic since the conflict with the Dreilore. Burning bodies flashed through her mind's eye. Could her lightning become just as devastating as her fire? "No," she muttered. "I don't think that would help."

Zirin approached her other side, saving her from explaining herself further. His curls were so black they appeared stained with ink, the sections around his face held back with a leather clasp. He wore a fur-lined coat. Elmerah was sure she had never seen him in anything else. "I have tried many times," he explained, "the fog won't budge, and yet my winds easily fill the sails. Perhaps we should wake Rissine."

"She's already awake," Rissine's voice sounded behind them.

Elmerah turned, looking her sister up and down, huddled in her emerald coat. "What are you doing up?"

Rissine's dark eyes narrowed. "I went to check on my *sister* in her cabin, and she was missing."

Elmerah wrinkled her nose. Rissine had been clucking around her like a mother hen since they first boarded the ship. "I'm not a child that needs to be checked on in the night."

"Apparently you are since you're up here instead of resting. You need to recover your strength."

"My strength is fine," she snapped.

"Perhaps we should focus on the fog," Alluin interrupted.

Zirin remained silent at Elmerah's other side.

Elmerah watched as Rissine looked past them all toward the fog, lifted one hand, then lightning struck.

She whipped around just in time to catch the edge of the light, illuminating dark tattered sails on a distant ship.

"Akkeri ship," Zirin stated blandly.

Elmerah's mouth went dry. She tried to peer through the fog, but with no more lightning, the ship was invisible. "Akkeri do not have magic, they could not have created this fog."

"Their High King does," Alluin countered. "As far as I know, he is the only one. If this fog is magical, he is upon that ship."

Elmerah put a hand on his arm. Alluin had been held hostage by Hotrath, and nearly didn't make it out alive. She would have killed the High King herself, but she was Egrin's prisoner at the time. "He must think we can lead him to Saida. Or maybe he believes she is still with us."

"We've no time for further discussion," Rissine snapped. "They will know that we have seen them. If they plan to move upon us, they will do it now."

Zirin crossed his arms and leaned his hips against the railing. His broad shoulders strained against his coat. "Do we fight, or flee?"

Rissine chewed her lower lip and narrowed her eyes, deciding. Her gaze darted to Alluin. "You have the most experience with the High King. What say you?"

Alluin shook his head. "He is clever. He would not

follow us without reason, but his ultimate goal is Saida, and she's not here."

Elmerah's thoughts raced. Hotrath wanted Saida alive to break the alleged curse of the Akkeri. If he thought her upon this ship, he would not attempt to sink them, but he would attempt to board and would likely kill anyone who wasn't her.

Rissine gazed in the direction of the Akkeri ship. "He has remained hidden for a reason. He must know by now that we don't have Saida. Either he follows in hopes we will lead him to her, or perhaps he plans to take us hostage to use against her. Either way, if he has magic, we may not be prepared for an altercation." She looked to Zirin. "Summon your winds. Tonight we flee. Hopefully we can lose them amongst the smaller islands."

Next she looked to Alluin. "Wake Isara. We may need her to nullify his magic." Finally, her eyes landed on Elmerah. "You, stay with me."

Elmerah scowled, but nodded as Alluin and Zirin rushed off. She had spotted islands nearby in the light of day. She knew those islands. If they could make it to one, she knew where to hide. "Do we try to sink his ship as we flee?"

Rissine gave her a calculating look. "You just stay with me. I will attack his ship once we have gained momentum."

Elmerah read in Rissine's eyes exactly what she was thinking. She was just as afraid of Elmerah's magic, just as worried that she would lose control.

Elmerah wrapped her arms tightly around herself, then followed Rissine as she led the way across the deck. The elves already awake ran to and fro, some jumping below deck to help Alluin wake the others.

Elmerah's fingers dug into each of her arms, straining her bandages. Her magic had never been overly strong, at least not for a Shadowmarsh witch. She had always trusted it, relied on it. To fear it was to fear an innate part of herself.

But if it came to it, if Hotrath caught up and tried to harm those she cared about, she would unleash it upon him. And Cindra help any who stood in her path.

Saida

Saida distantly felt the cool sand beneath her back, and Malon gripping her hand as the curse took her. Darkness consumed her, and then she was on her feet, walking through the sand alone. She hugged herself, rubbing her hands up and down her arms. The ritual had worked, and now she was stuck in a dark place, just like when Urali had cursed her.

Or maybe not exactly the same. This darkness was less oppressive, less suffocating. The sand beneath her feet transitioned to stone as she continued walking.

Stars glittered overhead, countless stars, more bright than she had ever seen. They lit her barren surroundings, and her fogging breath. The stones she tread upon stretched out endlessly into the darkness.

She went over Brosod's instructions. Her first instinct would be to panic. She was trapped in this dark place alone, but she had to remember she wasn't really here. It was something like a dream. Once she found Elmerah, she would be able to return to her body. She would also return if she ran out of time and sunlight came. Those were the terms of the curse.

Now, to simply find Elmerah. Still hugging herself tightly, she stopped walking, closed her eyes, and focused on her friend. She thought of her bluster, her wry wit, and her unwavering loyalty. She thought of the last time she saw her, bravely fighting demons in Skaristead. It seemed so very long ago.

A shift in her perception made her eyes fly wide. She sensed a spark off in the distance. A spark that felt like Elmerah. Brosod had explained that even if Elmerah was far away, Saida should be able to travel to her quickly, as long as she focused intently on her friend's energy.

She hurried across the stones, soon spotting a distant fire.

"I see he tricked you into working a curse," a voice said behind her.

The toe of her boot caught on one of the stones and she went sprawling across the hard surface. Her mind screaming with panic, she rolled over and staggered to her feet, facing that voice. Egrin Dinoba's voice.

The demon emperor stood only a few paces away, his arms crossed within his fine black coat, embroidered with gold and silver. His black pants were plain, his legs encased up to his knees in tall, freshly polished boots. Finally, she reached his eyes, cold, calculating blue eyes. His black hair was a bit longer than the last time she'd seen him, though still shorter than what most men of high station chose.

She waited for his magic to hit her, to steal the air from her lungs.

"I'm not here to harm you," he said. "I'm not really here at all. This is your curse, your dream. I am merely a visitor."

She lifted a hand toward her brow, but the Crown of Cindra was not there. It was on her body, lying prone in the sand somewhere far away with Malon and the others. "What do you want?" she asked, lowering her hand.

"I've come to remind you of our bargain. The full moon is not far off. Don't you want to save your people?"

If she told him she had no intention of bringing him the circlets, would he turn on her? Would he obliterate Faerune without a second thought?

The corner of his mouth curled into something between a smile and a sneer. "A bargain with one of my kind is binding. I will not destroy your people until the full moon, and if you bring me the circlets, what remains of Faerune will be spared entirely. I will never turn my sights toward them again."

She took a long breath to still her trembling. "And once you have the circlets? What then?"

"That is none of your concern."

She watched him warily, debating whether she should run. The curse would only last so long, and she needed to find Elmerah. "I'll consider your offer," she lied.

He laughed. "I am as old as this land. Do you think I cannot read a lie on someone so young? If only I could pass this skill on to you, you would realize how Malon has manipulated you."

He's a demon, she thought. *Don't believe a word he says.*

He took a step toward her. "Ask him what deal he made with me. Ask him why he was willing to let the Dreilore into Faerune. He could have stolen the Crown of Arcale some other way. Ask him why it had to be *that* way."

He lifted his hand, snapped his fingers, then disappeared in a cloud of darkness, leaving her alone with nothing but the stars.

She took a long moment to catch her breath, staring at the space where he had been. Was she a fool to trust Malon after all he had done? She needed Elmerah's help now more than ever. With a silent prayer to Cindra, she turned toward that distant fire and ran for all she was worth.

Rissine

Just as Zirin's winds began to whip through the sails, the fog cleared, revealing the imposing silhouette of the Akkeri ship. *Much* nearer than it was before. Rissine and Elmerah stood near the base of the main mast while elves hurried around them. Their ship picked up speed, whipping Rissine's loose hair around her face, but the Akkeri ship sped faster. In the moonlight she could see hunched forms skittering across the distant deck. Akkeri readying themselves to go to battle. Any hope she'd had that they would not attack was quickly quashed.

She turned as Alluin and Isara reached them, the latter clinging to her spectacles to keep them from being torn off her nose by Zirin's magical winds.

Isara pushed her wild curls back from her face with her other hand, looking to Rissine. "What would you have me do!" she shouted over the wind.

Rissine gripped the mast to steady herself as she pointed toward the Akkeri ship. "Can you nullify the High King's magic while still allowing me to rain lightning upon them?"

Isara glanced at the ship, then turned back toward Rissine with her brow furrowed. "I can try!"

With a quick glance at Elmerah, who was being uncharacteristically quiet, Alluin took Isara's arm and helped her make her way toward the ship's railing. Celen joined them, taking hold of Isara's other arm to keep her steady. Unfortunately, he would be otherwise useless. Calling the earth did little good out at sea.

Rissine turned toward Elmerah. "If you're not up for this, I can handle the attack."

Elmerah's eyes were too wide. Her shortened hair whipped in the wind, a blatant reminder of her almost burning herself alive. "I can do this! Only lightning, no fire."

But could her lightning get just as out of control? Would she sink their ship while trying to sink the Akkeri's? Rissine didn't have to consider long. The risk was too great. "Just watch my back for now. I'll take care of the ship."

Elmerah watched her for a moment, then gave a sharp nod.

Rissine led the way toward the railing as Isara lifted her arms into the air. More of the fog cleared. The Akkeri ship seemed to slow. She was just close enough to hear Isara cry, "I cannot hold him off for long! He's too far away!"

Rissine reached for her rapier, wanting the tool to guide her magic more precisely. If Isara could only nullify the High King's magic when he was close, he would be able to catch up again as soon as they gained any distance. She withdrew her rapier and pointed it toward the sky. She would need to strike now, while she still could.

Thunder rumbled, and the air became thick with the pressure of a storm. She could sense Elmerah standing close to her back, doing nothing, which was so horribly unlike her it had Rissine worried about more things than just Elmerah's uncontrollable magic.

Her lightning struck down, hitting the center of the ship with absolute precision, then bouncing off harmlessly. Her jaw fell open.

"I don't know how he did that!" Isara cried. "His magic should be nullified!"

And it was true. They were gaining more distance on the Akkeri ship. Perhaps if Isara could just nullify him long enough, and with the help of Zirin's winds, they might be able to escape without damaging the other ship. Her blood ran cold at the sound of a distant cannon.

"Zirin!" she shouted, hoping he was close enough to hear her. The rain from her summoned storm began to fall, the heavy droplets echoing across the ocean.

A heartbeat later Zirin's winds left the sails empty, turning to gust in the direction of the Akkeri ship just as the cannonball came crashing toward them. It fell harmlessly into the dark sea below, just as another one fired. Without Zirin's wind in the sails, the Akkeri ship began to gain on them even without magic.

"If they reach us we'll be overwhelmed!" Alluin shouted.

Another cannonball fired and was repelled. While the Akkeri could not have an unlimited supply of ammunition, Zirin also did not have an unlimited supply of magic.

Rissine reached back and took Elmerah's hand. "We have to take them out! *Now.*"

She looked back to see Elmerah shaking her head, her eyes wide with panic. Rain streamed down her face, soaking her hair. "I can't," she rasped.

"Oh Ilthune take us all," Rissine growled. She grabbed Alluin's arm, then placed Elmerah's hand in his. "Take care of her."

As he stepped back toward Elmerah, Rissine took his place at Isara's side. She glanced toward the demon-blooded woman, her wet foggy spectacles obscuring her eyes. "Is nullifying magic all you can do?"

Isara gritted her teeth. "Yes, and I can only manage it for so long."

Celen placed a hand on Isara's shoulder and looked past her toward Rissine, his dripping wet features grim. "If we don't do something, they'll reach us. We must be prepared to fight."

Her fingers flexed around her rapier. How many Akkeri could she claim before her ship was overwhelmed. She understood Elmerah's panic, but without her, the sea or the Akkeri would claim them all.

Elmerah

Elmerah's entire body trembled—she couldn't seem to control it. She had collapsed to her knees upon the swaying deck, slick with rainwater, with Alluin crouched by her side.

"I can't do it," she panted. "I reached for my magic and it did not answer." She closed her eyes, seeing flames and burning bodies in her mind.

Alluin took her hand, squeezing it lightly through her wet bandages. "It's alright, let Rissine handle it."

The ship lurched in the wind, sending her wet hair flicking forward into her face. She closed her eyes and reached again for her magic, and nothing answered. Fear closed around her heart. What if she couldn't stop her fire, and it consumed their ship? As much as she tried to push the thought away, it plagued her. It plagued her so completely that as hard as she tried, her magic would not come.

She felt Alluin's free hand brushing her forehead, pushing her wet hair back from her face. She pinched her eyes more tightly shut. Curse it all, she was going to get him killed. She couldn't let that happen.

She squeezed Alluin's hand, then staggered to her feet, blinking back tears. She was glad for the rain dampening her face, she couldn't let anyone see her cry. If she couldn't use her magic, she would simply have to use her blade.

Alluin stood at her side, and they both watched as the Akkeri ship drew near. The sound of the first arrows flying cut through the roaring sea and rain.

CHAPTER TWO

Saida

Saida ran like an arrow true to its target, straight toward that distant fire that she knew was her friend. Her legs never seemed to tire as she traveled across land and sea. Finally, the fire grew near, and figures materialized before her eyes.

She was on a ship, accosted by pounding rain and violent winds. Beyond the ship she could see dark islands like smudges of ink against the foggy night sky. It took her a moment to make sense of things. Elves with bows ran toward the railing on one side of the ship, none of them able to see her. Arrows flying from another ship sailed straight toward the deck, only to be cast away by the winds. *Magical winds*. She searched the deck, spotting the tall Arthali directing them.

Finally, her eyes landed on Elmerah and Alluin, and her heart sank. Elmerah lay flat on the deck while Alluin prepared to remove an arrow from her shoulder.

Saida ran toward them, reaching out, but she couldn't touch them, nor could they see her. She had to figure out just where they were, and where they were going so she could find them in the waking world.

Someone ran so close they nearly went through her, and she realized as he passed that it was Merwyn. He ran toward Rissine, who stood near the railing with her rapier drawn. Next a young male Nokken ran past. She was so stunned she stumbled backward. Why in the gods was a Nokken on board?

Saida tore her eyes away from him, then moved forward and crouched down beside Elmerah and Alluin. Vail, the healer Saida had originally met at a Valeroot settlement, joined them, her eyes intent on the arrow piercing Elmerah's shoulder. The rain washed her blood across the deck in bursts of crimson.

"Pull it out!" Elmerah grunted. "I need to help my sister!" Her eyes were wild and frantic like a cornered animal.

Vail yanked the arrow out and Elmerah screamed.

Alluin held her down. He had removed his wet cloak to press against her wound. "We need to get you below deck. You've lost too much blood."

Vail had already run off to tend the other wounded.

Saida stood helplessly by. More arrows sailed toward them. A gust of wind sent most of them into the sea, but a few cut through to thunk into the deck. They were answered by a flurry of elven arrows, sailing off into the darkness. Screams and squeals from the other ship cut across the waves.

The animalistic squeals made her breath catch. The other ship held Akkeri. She peered through the rain and mist toward the main mast of the other ship, where one much larger figure stood. His reflective eyes peered directly toward her. Hotrath, High King of the Akkeri, had spotted his intended prey.

Alluin now had Elmerah on her feet. She lifted her cutlass toward the sky, but no lightning answered.

Canon fire sounded, then the whole ship shook. Elmerah lost her footing and went skidding across the deck with Alluin diving after her. Saida searched for the Arthali controlling the winds and spotted him on the deck with an arrow in his thigh.

Another cannonball struck, echoed by screams. "Abandon ship!" an elf shouted.

Saida stood by helplessly as the ship began to sink. She couldn't spot Alluin and Elmerah in the chaos. Then suddenly she was sinking too, sinking down into darkness. Cold air tore through her lungs as she woke with a gasp, then sat up in the sand.

Malon braced her shoulder, keeping her upright. "What happened, did you find her?"

Tears streamed down her face as she glanced

around at the waiting Makali, all eyes on her. The few other elves in her party were gathered together, but slightly off on their own, watching with worry clear in their expressions. She turned away from the fire, away from all those waiting eyes. "Take me to my tent," she sobbed.

Malon scooped her up in his arms, carrying her like a child away from the Makali. Brosod followed toward the tents.

"Go back and tell them the curse was successful," he ordered. "We don't want to lose their faith."

With a quick nod, Brosod hurried back toward the fires.

With Brosod gone, Saida turned her face against Malon's chest and tried to focus on her breathing. She had to remain calm. She had to tell Malon what happened so they could find Elmerah and help her.

Because an arrow and a sinking ship couldn't be enough to take down her friend. It simply couldn't. She had to be alive. Alluin was with her, he would've gotten her to safety. She had spotted islands when she first arrived on the ship. He would have gotten her to one of those islands.

Malon carried her inside her tent and set her down on her sleeping mat.

She sat up, wiping the tears from her eyes. Her hands shook so violently she had to force them together into her lap. "We must go to Elmerah immediately. She needs our help."

He braced her shoulders, gazing steadily into her eyes. "Saida, I need you to tell me what happened."

Her words tumbled out like a babbling stream. She told him of her experience, starting with when she reached the ship.

When she finished, he stared at her for a long moment.

"We have to go to her, Malon."

He released his hold on her shoulders and sat back on his heels. "Saida, she might be dead, and we have less than two weeks to kill the emperor. Would you risk all of Faerune to search for your friend?"

Her throat went tight as more tears threatened. She shook her head, grasping for words. "There has to be a way to reach her quickly. Another curse. Find Brosod and ask her, we cannot waste another moment."

"Saida," Malon said patiently. "The Makali don't have that sort of power. They may be able to walk the dream world, but they cannot create portals."

She leaned forward, closer to him. "Then the circlets. We'll use the power of the circlets. There has to be a way."

He let out a long sigh, his reflective eyes shining bright in the dim lamplight. "You're not going to let this go, are you?"

"Elmerah is shipwrecked and wounded. How could I ever let that go? She needs saving, Malon, and so do all the others on that ship."

He shook his head. "There is a way, but it's risky. If

we go there, we may never make it back out. All of our work will be for nothing."

She leaned forward a little more, close enough to feel his breath on her skin. "Tell me."

He met her eyes. "There are many demon portals now throughout the land. I can sense them when they are near. If we enter one, we can use it as a means of travel to reach a far off area quickly."

Her heart sputtered like a dying flame. Was this truly her only option? To go *into* a demon portal? "But won't there be many demons inside?"

He nodded. "Yes, but even Egrin fears what we can do with the circlets, and he is their king."

She considered his words. She knew he had summoned demons before, so had he created some of these portals? "Malon," she began cautiously, "how is it that you can sense demon portals?"

His gaze lowered toward her hands in her lap. It was like she could feel him putting up more walls to keep her out.

"Tell me," she demanded. "If we are truly in this together, I deserve to know."

"I was born with demon blood in my veins," he admitted, his gaze still lowered. "It's more common than you think. Egrin was not the first demon to come to this land."

Her breath caught. She glanced him over. He looked like any other pure blooded Faerune elf. "And that's why you have magic? Why you can summon demons?" *Why you can use the circlet,* she added internally. Wasn't it inherently wrong to have the Crown of Arcale wielded by someone with demon blood?

When he still wouldn't look at her, she lifted one hand from her lap and pressed a finger underneath his chin.

He met her eyes reluctantly, as if afraid of what he might find there. He spoke before she could straighten out her thoughts. "Do not forget, Isara Saredoth also has demon blood, and you would make her empress."

She lowered her hand, considering him. He had his faults—and they were *many*—but in her heart she did not believe he was evil, at least not anymore. "Where is the nearest portal? How quickly can we reach Elmerah?"

He stared at her for a moment, then slowly blinked. "That is all you have to say?"

"If your demon blood can help us save my friend, then I will not fault you for it."

He crossed his legs beneath him and moved a little closer. "It will be dangerous, I cannot guarantee that we won't encounter a greater demon, but with the circlets we should be able to fend them off. Once we reach the portal, we can travel to Elmerah within a few days, perhaps less."

A few days. She did not want to accept it as good enough, but it was better than weeks. "And this is the only way to reach her quickly?"

"I would not suggest it if there were any other option.

In the meantime we can have the Makali march toward the Capital. We will lose no time on our quest."

She had nearly forgotten about the Makali in her panic. "Perhaps it would be better to send them to Faerune. They could protect it should we run out of time."

He put a hand on her arm. "Saida, we have agreed to kill the emperor. That is our plan. Once we have Elmerah, we will re-join with our army and march on Galterra."

She licked her dry, cracked lips, thinking of her meeting with Egrin. She could protect Faerune. She didn't have to rely on this wild plan. But if she gave the emperor the circlets, then what? Could she doom the rest of the land to protect her father and her home?

"How soon do we go to the portal?"

Malon seemed almost in pain at her answer, and she wondered just how bad going through a demon portal would be. She didn't have to wonder much. She had seen the Ayperos and the giant boars, and they were just lesser demons. They would surely run afoul of things *far* worse.

Movement caught her eye beyond Malon. She looked up as the tent flap opened, and Brosod peered in.

"We require privacy," Malon snapped at her.

Despite his words, Brosod stepped into the tent, letting the flap fall shut behind her. "I would ask that you bring me with you on this quest."

Malon stood abruptly to face her. "You were eaves-dropping?"

Brosod bowed her head. "Forgive me, I overheard."

Saida climbed to her feet, placing a hand on Malon's elbow to stop whatever he would say next. She looked past him toward Brosod. "Why would you want to venture into a demon portal?"

Brosod lifted her gaze. "You are the only people who can bring life to the desert. If you went into this portal and perished, and I could have done something to stop it—"

"You know nothing of demons," Malon interrupted. "You would simply be someone extra to protect."

Brosod lifted her chin proudly. "I am a hunter. I have hunted all my life. And I am a better tracker than either of you could ever hope to be. I can be useful."

Saida squeezed Malon's arm before he could continue lecturing Brosod, then she shook her head at her friend. "Brosod, you do realize how dangerous this mission is?"

Brosod nodded sharply. "I am not afraid of death. If this is what you must do to rescue your friend, I will help you in any way I can."

"Fine," Saida decided. "You can come."

Malon let out an irritated huff. "You are absolutely impossible."

She wasn't sure whether he was talking about her, or Brosod. Probably both.

"We must begin preparations immediately," he went

on. "I believe there is a portal near Fallshire. I will gather supplies there, and we will detail the route which our army must travel."

Saida nodded, though inside, her gut twisted. Fallshire was not far from Faerune, but they did not have the time to go to Faerune. They did not have the time to go and check if Egrin had kept his promise. If there was even anything left to save.

Brosod stepped back toward the tent flap. "I will go to the clan leaders. What would you have me tell them?"

Malon considered for a moment. "Tell them that once we reach Fallshire, the three of us are going to scout ahead. They may not react well to us using a demon portal."

Brosod nodded. "Yes, they would think us mad." She stepped out into the darkness, letting the tent flap fall shut behind her.

"They would think us mad," Malon sighed. "And they would be right."

Saida remained quiet, thinking once again of her conversation with Egrin. She could not fully dismiss the possibility that Malon was manipulating her, but in this new deal, she simply could not see how that might be. For what might Malon gain by entering a demon portal? All he stood to gain by helping her, was death.

Alluin

"Where is my sister?" Elmerah groaned over the sound of rain and lapping water.

She lay flat on her back on a piece of wood from the ship while Alluin paddled them toward the nearest island. He could see nothing below him in the dark sea, and all around the loudest sound was the waves.

"I'm sure she's fine," he consoled, his breath coming out in harsh pants, fogging the air before him. "I saw her jump ship before it went down."

"But the Akkeri," Elmerah muttered.

Judging by her weak voice, she was about to lose consciousness. "I need you to stay awake, Elmerah. We are almost there."

He could see the shore not far off. Distant tall trees swayed in the light of the half moon. He had no idea what the island might hold, but it was their only option. They had lost track of everyone else. It was impossible to see if there were any other survivors amongst the waves, but hopefully those who still lived would make it to the same island.

"The Akkeri," Elmerah said again, her voice barely audible over the choppy waters. "Where did they go after they sunk us?"

"I don't know," he huffed, the cold air burning his tired lungs with every inhale. "Don't worry about it now. Just talk to me about something else, keep yourself awake." He was terrified that if she drifted off, she would not wake again.

He couldn't say how much blood she had lost, and the water was so cold he worried he might not even make it to shore.

"It's my fault," she lamented. "It's my fault this happened. When I tried to reach for my magic, I froze. I was too afraid."

He pulled himself further onto the board, closer to her. "Afraid?" he asked. It was difficult to speak with his heaving breaths and chattering teeth, but he needed to keep her going.

"After what I did to the Dreilore. I couldn't control it. Couldn't control my fire. I'm so frightened that it will happen again. I was worried I would sink the ship myself."

He remembered her wide eyes, the fear shining so clearly when she tried to summon her magic. He hadn't realized what she did to the Dreilore affected her so deeply. "They would have sunk us either way," he soothed. *Just keep kicking your feet*, he told himself. *We'll get there*. "Their ship was immune to your sister's magic. There was nothing you could have done."

"My sister," she muttered, her voice faint.

"She's fine. She's a survivor." *Just a little further. We'll reach land and we'll get warm, then we'll find the others.* Vessa was a survivor too. She would make it. She had to.

"Alluin?"

He snapped back to the present. "I'm here. We've almost reached the shore."

"You were so quiet, I was afraid you were gone."

He would have given anything in that moment to hear her make a joke. She was never this candid. "I won't leave you. Now you need to hold on tight. The waves near shore will be rough."

She went quiet then, or maybe he just couldn't hear her over the water. He kicked his legs, his toes entirely numb. *Almost there.*

The waves whipped his body, nearly tearing him away from Elmerah. He clung to the board, his breath raging in his lungs, and continued to kick.

And just like that, they were beyond the rough waves. His boots hit sand. He used his new foothold to propel Elmerah the rest of the way toward shore.

Once she was secure, he rolled onto his back in the sand, the surf still lapping at his legs. He wasn't sure how long he lay there, trying to catch his breath, but the next thing he knew, Elmerah was standing over him, dragging him the rest of the way out of the water.

He managed to get to his feet, then nearly fell, but Elmerah kept him standing. And he kept her standing. Together, they staggered further inland, then both collapsed onto the sand.

He stared up at the glittering stars. Any hint of the Akkeri fog was gone, as was Rissine's storm. The night shone bright and clear before him. The stars were almost dizzying. "We need to get warm, I can't feel my hands or feet."

Elmerah's hand shifted across the sand, weakly

patting his shoulder. "I know a place where we can go, if we can manage to walk."

"Are you as delirious as I feel? We are on a remote island. How can you know a place?"

She struggled to sit up in the sand, leaning heavily on her uninjured arm. "I'm exhausted, and bleeding, and mad as a whipfish, but I know exactly where we are."

He sat up and looked at her, still not comprehending. "How can you possibly know where we are?"

She rolled her tired eyes. Her skin was sickly pale. "Because this is the island I escaped to when I first fled my people. I was living here before Rissine had me kidnapped and brought to the Capital."

His jaw fell open. "Are you sure?"

She nodded. "I'll need to start walking to find my bearings, but I recognize this shore. If we start walking now, we may find shelter before the night is through."

"And what about the others?"

She watched him for a moment, her indecision clear. "We all must have one priority for tonight. Get warm, and don't get caught by the Akkeri. We can't make a fire anywhere they might see."

"Are you strong enough to walk?" he asked, doubting his own abilities.

"I'm going to have to be."

Isara

Isara collapsed upon the dark shore while her brother remained standing, but just barely. He looked down at her, his expression unreadable as water dripped steadily from his hair and clothing.

She sat up, still trying to catch her breath, then removed her spectacles to shake off the droplets clouding her vision. It was a miracle she had managed to keep them on her face during the long swim. Her brother's gaze was heavy upon her. "Why are you looking at me like that?"

"Honestly, I'm surprised you didn't let me go down with the ship. As soon as I heard the chaos above, I thought for sure I would be forgotten."

Her jaw hung open. For him to think she would even consider leaving him behind, or that she would forget entirely . . . she shook her head. Daemon had never understood her, nor she him. As soon as her allies had started jumping ship, she had risked her life running below deck to free Daemon from the brig. It was only luck that had her easily finding the keys hanging from a hook on the wall. And even acting swiftly, they had barely made it up to the deck while it was still above water. By the time they jumped into the sea, her allies were all just shadows in the water swimming toward the distant isles. She had lost track of them as soon as she hit the cold water, and any thoughts beyond survival had left her.

She could only hope they had all made it.

Daemon watched her for a moment longer, then offered her his hand. She took it and stood, her legs feeling wobbly like thistle jelly. While she was relatively fit from farm work and traveling, she had never been a strong swimmer. If Daemon hadn't pulled her along half the way, she never would have made it. He could talk about being forgotten all he wanted, when it came right down to it, he'd refused to leave her behind, even if he risked drowning himself.

He dropped her hand and observed their dark surroundings. There was no sign of life on the shore, and the shadowy trees leading inland seemed ominous.

"We should seek shelter," Daemon decided. "Now that we are away from your witches, I'm sure Egrin will find us."

She gasped, stepping back until her boots were in the surf. "Does he have a way of locating you?"

Daemon smirked. "He can locate anyone. I do not know why you continue to labor against him."

"He's a demon," she hissed, though she knew the argument would fall on deaf ears. They'd had it many times already while he was locked in the brig.

"And your *friends* are Shadowmarsh witches. It's debatable which one is worse."

She crossed her trembling arms. She needed a fire and to be out of her wet clothes, but she could not let the conversation go. "Those witches are the bravest women I've ever met."

Ignoring her, Daemon started wringing water out of his dripping wet locks. Without the use of an iron to straighten them, they would be just as curly as Isara's, something Daemon didn't want anyone to know. It gave her a small amount of satisfaction that whoever saw them next would see the true texture of Daemon's hair. His ridiculous, long-guarded secret would be out.

"Fine," she huffed. "Let us seek shelter. Elmerah and Rissine are likely somewhere on this same island. If Egrin comes, I will nullify his magic long enough for them to come kill him."

Daemon flicked the water off his hands. "You sound like a child."

"And you act like one," she grumbled, and started walking.

They walked down a path within the trees, and didn't have to go far before they found a small abandoned shelter. Even with just the short walk, Isara's legs were fully prepared to give out beneath her.

Hands on hips, Daemon observed the shelter with a look of distaste. "This will have to do for the night. Judging by how easily we found something man-made, this must be an inhabited island. We'll search for civilization in the morning."

We will search for my friends whether you like it or not, Isara thought. *Even if I have to drag you.* Scowling at her brother's back, she followed him into the shelter, which was little more than four walls with no door. The thatched roof overhead showed the trees above in several places. She shivered just thinking about how much cold air the holes would let in, not to mention the missing door.

Daemon glanced around the dark interior, then plopped down upon the hard-packed dirt floor. He looked up at his sister. "You're shivering. I'd offer you my coat, but—" he gestured down to his sopping wet clothing.

She was utterly exhausted, but the sea water had been icy, and she couldn't let herself freeze in the night after all she had gone through. "I'll find materials for a fire."

"We have no fire-striker."

She couldn't help but lift her nose a bit into the air. "While you sat getting pampered in Galterra, I was traveling on my own. We will have a fire soon, but we should keep it small in case the Akkeri are searching for us."

Daemon crossed his arms and leaned back against the wall. "I'll believe it when I see it."

Isara stalked back out into the night, intent on proving her brother wrong, in more ways than one.

Daemon

Daemon sighed as he stared into the embers of their small fire, Isara fast asleep across from him. Foolish girl had gotten lucky . . . though he was eternally grateful for the fire.

Unable to sleep, he got up and went outside to relieve himself. He wouldn't go far. As vexing as she was, he wasn't about to let any Akkeri kidnap his sister.

He went further down the small path, then off into a copse of trees. He was about to undo his breeches when he sensed a presence beside him. When he turned, he wasn't surprised to see Egrin leaning calmly against the nearest tree.

With arms crossed, he looked Daemon up and down. "I'm surprised to see you're still alive."

Daemon straightened his shoulders, then brushed imaginary lint from his fraying sleeve. "It's about time you came for me. Although you could have come while I was locked in the brig of that ship."

Egrin smirked. "Now why would I do that when having you taken hostage was so convenient?"

Daemon turned to fully face Egrin, crossed his arms, then leaned against the nearest tree. "Something tells me I'm not going to like what you're about to say."

Glancing in the direction of the shelter where Isara still slept, Egrin stepped closer and lowered his voice, "I don't care if you like it. Here is what you're going to do."

CHAPTER THREE

Alluin

Alluin was up before the sun, rifling through the abandoned supplies in the small home. *Elmerah's home*. He could hardly imagine her living in such a place, all alone. The wooden walls were thin, the furniture sparse. At least there had been some dry clothing for her to wear, and bandages for her arrow wound. But no silverleaf sap.

They would need to find a way to disinfect her wound before infection could set in. With the remaining bandages, he had rewrapped the worst of her burns, which would heal more slowly now without Vail's salve.

With a heavy sigh, he continued his perusal of her belongings, noting hints of her personality here and there. There were a few gathered shells on the windowsill, and other bits and bobs she must have found along the coast. He pictured her in this place, alone, hiding from her past. He couldn't imagine what it must have felt like. Even in his darkest moments, he'd always had his clan, and once they were lost, he'd had Elmerah.

He glanced toward her, still asleep on the small bed as the sun began to rise. Her new coat was pale gray, stained in some places, but warm. Her breeches were black, like what she usually wore, topped by the black boots she'd slept in, just in case they had to flee quickly. She had offered him the coat first since he had lost his cloak, but he was more worried about her staying warm, and the coat wouldn't have fit across his shoulders regardless.

He froze at the sound of movement outside, and whispers. He glanced at the bed, finding Elmerah's eyes now open.

She sat up and looked over her shoulder, her attention on the door.

Alluin lifted a finger to his lips, and she nodded. The only weapon they had was the dagger at Alluin's belt, everything else had been lost to the sea. Elmerah had made no further mention of her magic since her admission while they were still laboring toward shore.

Clutching his dagger, he crept toward the door, then pressed his back against the wall directly next to it. The door swung open, and he whipped the dagger out, placing it against Celen's throat.

Celen didn't move except to lift his hands in surrender. He looked past Alluin toward Elmerah now climbing off the bed. "Not quite the greeting I was expecting."

Alluin lowered the dagger, allowing Celen to step inside. Merwyn waited just behind him.

Elmerah looked them both up and down. "And just how did you two end up together?"

Celen smirked, wrinkling the scars on one side of his face. His fur-lined coat was mostly dry now, and torn at one shoulder. "We found each other on shore. We haven't managed to locate any of the others. I imagine they all journeyed inland to hide, just like you two." He glanced around the small space. "At least you happened upon nicer accommodations. We both spent the night asleep in the dirt."

"We got lucky," Elmerah said, giving Alluin a warning look.

He didn't have time to ponder why Elmerah wouldn't want Celen to know this place used to be her home. She walked past him and out the door, calling back, "Come along!"

Alluin shrugged at Celen and Merwyn, then followed her out.

Birds sang happily overhead in the tall trees, rejoicing in a bit of unclouded sunlight. Elmerah was looking further east, down an overgrown path. He stepped up to her side.

She pointed in the direction she'd been peering.

"There is a small port that way. If we're lucky, there will be a ship docked there. Once we find the others we can barter passage to the mainland, although I don't know what we could possibly use to trade. Perhaps Rissine has managed to keep hold of her coin purse."

Celen and Merwyn joined them. "Will they take kindly to Arthali?" Celen asked.

Elmerah shrugged, though she had been to the town before, she should know how folk would react. "Only one way to find out." She looked over to Merwyn. "You, however, should remain hidden. Do you think your High King will search for us?"

Merwyn's already saggy skin drooped further as he lowered his chin. "He seeks Saida. If he believes we can lead him to her, he will not give up so easily."

Elmerah considered him for a moment. "Do you know why my sister's magic bounced harmlessly off his ship?"

Merwyn nodded, but it was Celen who explained, "All of the bolts and nails are made of Dreilore metals. It's quite brilliant if you ask me. It makes the entire ship immune to magical attacks."

"Yes, brilliant," Elmerah said caustically. She flexed her bandaged hands. "We should get walking. If Hotrath is to catch us, I'd rather it occur in a town where there will be plenty of distractions." She turned and started walking down the path.

Alluin watched her go for a moment.

Celen leaned in near his shoulder. "Is she alright?"

"I don't think so," he muttered, then started walking.

He wished Celen and Merwyn had not found them so soon. Elmerah had finally let down a wall within herself the night before, but as soon as the pair showed up it had slammed back into place. He wasn't sure when he would get the opportunity to see it down again. He found he had many things he still wanted to say to her, and hoped she would find it in herself to listen.

Rissine

Rissine woke up the next morning with a spear at her throat. At the other end of the spear was an Akkeri, its sickly, sallow skin adorned with mismatched pieces of armor, probably stolen from its victims. She wrinkled her nose at the strong fishy smell coming from the creature, knowing there would surely be more nearby. There always were.

The spear tip pressed against her throat as the creature said something in its language.

"I don't speak Akkeri." She sucked her teeth, debating how best to end the creature.

Something large moved to her side, blocking out the harsh rays of morning sunlight. She turned her head, careful not to slice her skin on the dirty spear.

The largest Akkeri she had ever seen loomed over her. He was just as grotesque as the rest, but instead of being skin and bones, strong muscles corded his arms beneath the pushed up sleeves of a silken tunic. *Like painting rouge on a pig,* she thought. The fine clothes looked out of place against his worm-like skin. Beyond him stood several more smaller Akkeri.

She rolled her eyes up to meet the large Akkeri's waiting gaze. She'd seen him once, but from a distance. "High King Hotrath, I presume?"

He grinned down at her. "Rissine Volund, witch of Shadowmarsh. You are lucky to be alive, for now."

His firm grasp on the common tongue took her aback. Her magic had already begun to well up within her, prepared to decimate the surrounding Akkeri, but perhaps it could wait a moment more. "What do you want? Why did you attack my ship?" She hesitated. "And what have you done with Zirin?" He was *supposed* to be keeping watch while she rested.

Hotrath crouched down beside her. "I want to know why Saida Fenmyar is in the Helshone. What is she planning?"

Her eyes widened. "I have absolutely no idea. You sunk my ship just to ask me that?"

He stood and turned his back on her. "I sunk your ship because the emperor wants you."

"You hope to turn me in?" She would strike them all down before she let that happen.

"No," he answered, his back still turned and arms

48

crossed. "I have worked with him before, and he betrayed me. He promised me a moon priestess. He promised me Saida." He shifted his weight, blinding her with the sun.

She squinted her eyes, trying to keep him in her sights. "Then you hope for revenge?"

He turned back to her, once more blocking out the sun. "Saida is my only concern. You will help me claim her, or I will hunt down your sister and turn you both in to Egrin Dinoba. The rest of your crew, any who still survive, will be killed."

Her magic welled at the threat.

Hotrath gestured to the Akkeri holding the spear at her throat, and the sharp tip pressed into her flesh. "I can sense your magic girl. Call it again and you're dead."

She counted backwards from ten to one in her head, reining in her temper. "How am I supposed to give you the priestess when she is in the middle of the Helshone?"

"She will not be there for long. In fact, she was on your ship last night. I saw her like a phantom, barely visible to the naked eye. She knows what has happened, I have no doubt she will come to the aid of her friends."

He was speaking utter gibberish—there was no way Saida had been upon her ship last night—but she wasn't in the habit of arguing with creatures who were on the verge of having her killed. "If you believe she is already coming here, then what do you need from me?"

"She possesses the Crown of Cindra," he explained. "I can sense it wherever it is. It once belonged to me. If she has learned how to use it, I will not risk facing her openly. You must take the circlet from her, and deliver both the priestess and the Crown of Cindra to me. Agree to this, and I will allow both you and your sister to escape." He crouched back beside her.

She narrowed her eyes at him. "There must be more to it than that. You would trust my word alone that I would aid you?"

He smiled indulgently, like he was speaking with a child. "Hardly. I would never trust the word of a Shadowmarsh witch. I would, however, trust her survival instinct. Help me, and I will stand with you against Egrin Dinoba, and any forces he sends your way. The numbers of my people are great. You would have a vast army at your disposal."

She knew regardless of what she decided, she would need to agree to his proposal here and now. She wasn't about to die due to simple pride. But . . . it wasn't a bad offer. She could have an entire army to protect Elmerah. That was, if Hotrath was a creature of his word.

He chuckled. By the look on his face, she almost wondered if he could read her thoughts. "You may have some time to think upon it." He removed a small trinket from around his neck, held on a thin silver chain. "Take this, and summon me when you are in need of an army. I will expect both the priestess and the circlet as payment." He leaned close, dangling the trinket in front of her face. It looked like a tiny silver whistle. "And know this, witch. The only reason I have not killed Dinoba is because I still hope to use him. Fail me, and your use will be at an end."

He leaned back, gesturing for the Akkeri to remove the spear from her throat.

Once she was free, she sat up and swiped the whistle from Hotrath's waiting hand. With her new vantage point she could see Zirin standing surrounded by Akkeri, five different spears pointed at his throat. The torn hem of his coat was wrapped around the arrow wound in his leg like a bandage.

"You were supposed to be standing watch," she hissed.

His onyx black hair had come loose to form tight curls around his face. He glared at her through those curls. "Forgive me for being tired after dragging your ass to shore."

Hotrath laughed, standing before stepping back amongst his people. He gestured for the spears surrounding Zirin to be lowered, though his unsettling gaze remained on Rissine. "Remember what we have discussed, witch. I make a far better friend than an enemy." With that, he turned away, and the other Akkeri followed.

Rissine debated summoning her magic and obliterating them all, but Hotrath was king for a reason. He had magic, and judging by the events of the previous night, he was strong.

Still clutching the silver chain affixed to the whistle,

she stood and looked to Zirin. "Let's find my sister and get out of here."

He watched her calmly with eyes as black as his hair, his bronze skin looking golden in the morning sun. "If you take the Akkeri's deal, she'll never forgive you."

"That's none of your concern," she growled, then turned to start walking.

She had made this choice once before, to protect Elmerah at all costs, even if it meant her sister would hate her. She could only hope it wouldn't come to that. If the elven priestess really could use the Crown of Cindra, she might be a lot more useful to Rissine than an army of Akkeri. That would be a choice to be made when the priestess came for them. If she came at all.

Saida

Saida waited south of Fallshire, seated upon a rock in a marshy forest. Luc and some of the other elves who'd survived the Helshone lounged nearby, keeping a close eye on her while pretending not to. There had been others waiting for them just outside the small village. Other elves like Phaerille and Luc, either of mixed-blood or betrayed in some way by Faerune. She hadn't expected there to be so many.

Even with the shock, she felt better to be so close to home, though she could not afford to visit. The Makali milled amongst the trees. While she didn't speak Kaleth, she could guess at what they were saying. Most of them had never seen so many tall trees in one place before, and the sprawling lush grasses drew much attention. Maybe they would change their minds about regrowing the desert, claiming the unprotected lands here instead.

She took a deep breath of the moist air, her gaze lingering in the direction of Fallshire. She and Malon had ventured in earlier that morning to obtain new clothing and supplies. Her simple breeches and soft gray tunic felt odd against her skin after wearing the flowing robes of the Makali. She had two daggers at her belt, and next to them, the circlet. She was always hesitant to touch it, hesitant to hear the whispers. She wasn't sure she ever wanted to learn what they had to tell her.

She stood. Malon would soon finish detailing a route for their army, and it would be time to go. But there was one last thing she knew she needed to do. Something she had been avoiding.

The Makali had kept guard over Phaerille, waiting for Saida to decide the fate of the traitor. The only issue was that she had no idea what to do. Phaerille had tried to have her killed—twice. She had lied and schemed, all the while pretending to be a true friend. If Phaerille had attacked her directly, perhaps she would have had the strength to kill her, but now—she simply wasn't in the habit of ordering executions. Even within Faerune, under the rule of the High Council, executions were exceedingly rare, the most severe punishment being exile.

She looked to Brosod, standing beneath the shade of a nearby tree, her eyes tilted upward as she marveled at the tall branches overhead. Oddly, the tan breeches and loose shirt two shades darker suited her, the fabric clinging to her well-muscled body. The clothes didn't look out of place at all, nor did her spear or the daggers at her belt. She had a bow and quiver slung across her shoulder too, so she could hunt for game should their journey take longer than expected.

Sensing Saida's attention, Brosod lowered her eyes from the branches. "You seem agitated."

Saida shrugged, wondering if Brosod was perhaps another wyrm in disguise. She didn't think so, but then again, she would never have thought such things of Phaerille. "I'm just wondering if we should do anything with Phaerille before we depart."

Brosod shrugged, the sunlight glinting off her short black hair. "She won't be harmed now that you have ordered it to be so. You can leave her behind without guilt."

"But we can't hold her prisoner indefinitely."

Brosod moved closer, her boots swishing through the grass. "Maybe she will be killed some other way and will save you the trouble."

She knew Brosod would gladly kill Phaerille herself

if only she would let her. Judgment within the desert was harsh, and exile was a crueler fate than a swift death.

She sighed. "Perhaps I should pay her a visit before we leave, to explain that she will be safe while we are away."

Brosod crossed her arms. "She deserves no such courtesy."

Saida couldn't quite meet her eyes. In truth, as much as Phaerille's betrayal had stung, all she felt for her was pity. Phaerille had been born from the forbidden union between a mother from Faerune, and a Valeroot hunter. She would never fit in with either clan, nor would she fit in amongst humans. She had seen Malon as her future, a chance to finally have a home, and she had loved him. In her eyes, Saida had taken him away, though in truth she had no romantic designs as far as Malon was concerned.

Brosod pursed her lips as she watched her. "I believe you waste too much energy on this traitor, but if you would like to see her before we leave, I will escort you."

Saida met Brosod's scrutinizing gaze for a moment, then looked down toward her boots. "I'm not sure what I would even say to her."

"You have not spoken with her since her betrayal. Perhaps you should let her do the talking."

She kicked around a pebble with her toe, halfway hoping Malon would return and tell her there was no time, that they must depart immediately. There really wasn't time. Who knew what state Elmerah was in now?

"Take me to her," she decided. "If I am to perish in the demon realm, I'd rather go without regrets."

Brosod lifted a dark brow. "That is not at all comforting." She turned to lead the way to where Phaerille was being kept amongst the Makali ranks.

Together they wove through the trees, and Saida's steps began to feel lighter as she went. The decision was made. She would hear whatever Phaerille had to say. She could sense Luc and the other elves following at a distance. She wondered if they would miss her once she was gone, and found, to her surprise, that she would miss them too. Nothing could form a bond faster than surviving near death together.

Malon emerged from a tent set up among the trees, quickly spotting her. He said something in Kaleth to the gathering of Makali still inside, then walked toward her. His clothing was all dark gray, matching her tunic. The color suited his silver hair and eyes better than it suited anything about her. She wondered if he had made them match intentionally, or if he had simply picked from whatever was available. She had waited in the nearby shadows while he chose, both of them fearful she might be recognized.

She realized she had stopped to wait for him without thinking about it, Brosod standing quietly behind her.

"We are almost ready to depart," he said as he reached them. "I just need to speak with a few more of the clan leaders. Where are you off to?"

"She wishes to speak with the traitor before we go,"

Brosod explained. "Just in case we die."

Saida gritted her teeth. Not exactly how she would have chosen to explain things.

Malon watched her for a moment, then nodded. "Isleth should be in the same direction. His clan took charge of her while we traveled." He started to turn away, then stopped. "But we should make this quick, or do you no longer care about reaching Elmerah in time?"

She glared at him. "*You're* the one that has been holding us up."

His eyebrow twitched, the only small hint that he was merely teasing her. "I am leaving my army behind for you, Saida. I would not leave them behind without proper orders. They should be able to travel mostly undetected with the route I have detailed, and if we time things right, we will have no trouble meeting up with them again."

She put her hands on her hips. "You've made your point, now let's get on with it."

He gave her a slight bow, then dramatically gestured for her to lead the way.

She did, her spine stiff and cheeks burning.

They passed many other tents well-hidden in the trees. The Makali would stay in this place one more night to hunt and gather any other food they could, then they would move on toward the Illuvian forests.

Saida's nerves caught up with her as they reached the tent where Phaerille was being held captive. Malon nodded to each of the Makali guards outside, then pushed aside the tent flap for Saida to enter ahead of him.

She looked a question at him. "You're coming with me?"

"She tried to have you killed once, I won't have you alone with her."

She glanced over her shoulder at Brosod.

Brosod wrinkled her nose. "I will wait out here, lest I become too tempted to kill her."

Saida nodded, squared her shoulders, then walked inside the tent. She involuntarily lifted a hand to her chest when she saw Phaerille, curled up on her side in the grass within the tent, her spirit broken. Her once lustrous honey blonde hair hung limp and dirty, covering half of her thin, pale face. Thick ropes bound her wrists, making them look frail. She still wore the robes of the Makali, as well as the bruises from the beating she had taken. Saida knew a little bit about bruises. Her ribs and abdomen still ached from what Urali had done to her, and the healing split in her lip still stung.

Phaerille blinked a few times, her eyes first landing on Saida, then settling on Malon. "Have you finally come to free me? I think I have been punished enough."

Saida's pity vanished like dandelion fluff on the wind. "Free you? You tried to have me killed."

Phaerille ignored her, her eyes still on Malon. "I served you loyally. I love you. You would not leave me here."

Saida turned her attention to Malon, wanting to judge his reaction.

He stared at Phaerille, his expression impassive. "You betrayed me at every turn. Why would I free you? Saida's kind heart is the only reason you still live."

Phaerille used her bound hands to push herself into a seated position. The expression on her face was frightening, like a priestess gazing at an idol of Cindra in utter devotion. "Anything I did, I only did because I love you." Her weak voice cracked, on the edge of tears.

Malon looked at her like she was an insect. "You know nothing of love. Your heart is selfish and weak. Saida will not let me kill you, but this will be the last time you ever see me."

Phaerille stared blankly for a moment, then began to cry in earnest.

Ignoring her, Malon looked to Saida. "If you have anything to say to her, now is your time."

Her jaw slightly agape, she just shook her head. She realized she wasn't the one who had needed to find closure with Phaerille. It was Malon who needed to say his final goodbye.

She glanced one last time at Phaerille, then turned back to Malon. "It doesn't matter. Once we have accomplished what we set out to do, we'll turn her loose, and neither of us will ever have to think about her again."

Phaerille's sobs followed them out of the tent, and Saida felt no pity at all.

CHAPTER FOUR

Alluin

Alluin's shoulders relaxed as the small port came into view, scented with woodsmoke from various cookfires. It had already been decided that he and Elmerah would search the town for the rest of their crew, while Celen and Merwyn kept an eye out near the shore further west. They had found a small stream to wash up and slake their thirst, but with torn clothing and injuries, they still looked like they had just come out of a battle.

Alluin walked at Elmerah's side as they ventured into the port. Most of the small town was built upon wooden docks, bordering a calm inlet of the sea. They passed a few elves and humans fishing off the docks with long poles, few paying them any heed. He noticed that some of the townsfolk possessed the darker coloring of the South, though everyone was deeply tanned regardless of heritage. His eyes widened as an older woman walked by, wearing a much shorter skirt than what he was used to seeing. He supposed on such a remote island, the people would make their own rules on what was and wasn't proper. Most of the men were shirtless, and the fabric they did wear was lightweight and dyed in deep earth tones.

He leaned in close to Elmerah as they reached a few small boats tethered to the dock. Too small to venture all the way to the mainland upon. "I can see why you chose to live here. There is an easy air about this place."

Elmerah turned toward the edge of the dock, gazing out across the glittering sea. She huddled within her stained gray coat, though the day was comfortably warm. "I did not *choose* to live here. Celen helped me smuggle myself onto a pirate ship, and this was the first place it docked. I figured it as good a place as any." She shrugged. "Of course, I was wrong. Rissine eventually found me."

He stood at her shoulder, looking back toward the sound of voices. A few fishermen had reached the dock on their small boat, and were talking loudly about finding a hot meal. He turned his attention to Elmerah. "Why didn't you want Celen to know?"

Her jaw tensed. "You mean this morning? It's humiliating. When he helped me escape Rissine, I told him I was going to do something great with my life. Something better than what I was born into. Then I got off at the first island and hid. I hid in that tiny shack and spent most of my time alone."

"It's not humiliating. You needed time to heal."

She shook her head, then turned to continue down the dock.

He caught up to her side, watching her dark eyes scanning across the people milling about. Soon they reached the end of the planks and veered onto a dirt path leading to some rickety wooden buildings with no doors. Inside the first one, a small man without a shirt stirred a massive boiling pot. A few men and women waited around with wooden bowls to be filled.

They walked down another path, then Elmerah turned to lean her back against a wall in the shade. "We will wait here. If any of our crew reach this place, they should walk down this main path."

Alluin leaned next to her, his thoughts still on their previous conversation. "You've done many great things since you left this island."

She watched the people walking by, her hair lifting in the breeze. He thought she might ignore him again, then finally, she asked, "Like what? It seems for all of our troubles we are still in the same place. Still trying to figure out a way to defeat the emperor. We have made no real progress."

He wasn't quite sure what to say to that. He thought of all they had been through. All of the failures, and few successes. "You know, that day I saw you at the inn—the first day we met—I was debating leaving Galterra for good."

She whipped wide eyes to him. "I don't believe you. Not after you and your uncle had worked so hard to protect your people."

He couldn't quite meet her eyes, but he knew he had to tell her. If she was willing to share her shame with him, the least he could do was grant her the same courtesy. "I was frustrated. We were always putting in the work, spying, trying to gain allies to survive. But we never seemed to get anywhere. Years went by, and we were still in the same place we had started. I was ready to be done with it all. If I couldn't create a life in Galterra, I would go somewhere else, perhaps even sail to an island far from the Capital."

She let out a rueful laugh and shook her head. "Then you saw an angry witch at a tiny inn and changed your mind?"

He smiled, recalling the memory. "I saw you and Saida together in a place where few Arthali or Faerune elves would dare to venture. At least not on their own. I took it as a sign that perhaps change had finally come. I knew I had to figure out who you were and what you were doing there."

The corner of her mouth ticked up. "And you got much more than you bargained for, didn't you?"

"What I got was my dearest friend, and my only shred of hope after my people had been slaughtered."

Her smile wilted. "I remember that night all too clearly," she said carefully.

He knew she was still waiting for him to talk about it. But what could he say? It had happened. It was done. There was no bringing them back. He watched a young couple passing by, laughing at some private joke. "I shouldn't have put so much pressure on you." He took a steadying breath. "I shouldn't have placed all of my hope in your hands. It wasn't your problem. None of it ever was."

She sidled a little closer to him, nudging her shoulder against his. "It's alright. It's not like I was doing anything else with my life. I only wish I could have been deserving of your faith." She leaned more heavily against the wall and gazed up at the sky. "Now look at me, wounded, beaten, and unable to even summon a lick of magic."

He'd thought about that too, why she was now so afraid, and why her magic had gone out of control to begin with. "Do you think—" he hesitated, unsure how she would take what he wanted to say.

She waited while a scantily-clad man carrying a line of fresh caught fish walked by, then said, "Go on."

He took a moment to choose his words. "Do you think your magic went so out of control because you were desperate to save Rissine? Because you knew she would be captured or killed if you didn't do something?"

A gust of salty breeze hit them. Elmerah lifted her chin and closed her eyes, inhaling deeply. "She wasn't the only one I was protecting. There was you, and Celen."

She opened her eyes and creased her brow. "Since finding you and Saida . . . it's the first time I really wanted to protect something after my mother was killed. I knew I could not fail. But what I did scared me more than anything else. If any of you had stood in the way of that magic, you would have been gone. I would have been helpless to control it." She shook her head. "I've never lost control like that."

He opened his mouth to say more, but Elmerah was peering in the other direction at a sandy-haired youth walking down the path. "Is that—"

"Killian," Alluin finished for her.

They pushed away from the wall and started walking.

The Nokken in disguise quickly noticed them, his eyes lighting up with excitement. He hurried forward, meeting them halfway down the path.

Alluin searched around, but saw no one else he recognized. "Are you here alone?" he asked Killian.

Killian pushed short hair away from his temporarily human face. "I reached shore not far from this place. I started searching for any of you this morning and only just returned here. Is Celen with you?"

"Keeping an eye out for the others near shore," Alluin explained. "Have you found anyone else? Isara? My sister—"

Killian shook his head. "No," he turned his attention to Elmerah, "*your* sister, however, I came across this morning, and you're not going to believe what I saw."

Elmerah's eyes went dark. "Let's start walking, we're

drawing attention." Once they were walking together down the path with Elmerah in the center, she asked, "Now what of my sister?"

"Well, she's alive," Killian began. "So is Zirin, they were together. But they were also meeting with a bunch of Akkeri. One of them was huge. That's how I found them to begin with. I could smell the Akkeri."

Elmerah had stopped walking. Her voice was cold and even, though Alluin could see the sudden fear in her eyes. "Did they capture her?"

Killian's eyes darted between her and Alluin. "Um, no. The giant Akkeri gave her something, and then they left. I wasn't close enough to see what it was. I followed Rissine and Zirin for a while, then they stopped to rest. Zirin has an injury."

"You didn't approach them?" Alluin asked.

Killian winced. "Forgive me, but after I saw them with the Akkeri . . . plus, Rissine is scary. She's so mean. Not like Elmerah."

Alluin caught a curious lingering glance from a man carrying a basket of fresh bread down the path. "We should find Celen and Merwyn and continue this conversation with them."

Elmerah nodded, her gaze distant.

Alluin didn't have to ask what she was thinking. She had never fully trusted her sister, and just what was she supposed to think now? Why would the Akkeri meet with her, but not capture her? Why had they really sunk their ship?

His stomach growled as they started walking, but he could hardly think of food. All he could think of was how he could possibly protect Elmerah. Arrows and Akkeri were one thing, but her own sister? He watched her out of the corner of his eye, but her expression gave nothing away. She had already taken a beating. She could withstand a great deal. But something told him if Rissine betrayed her again, it might be the thing to finally shatter her.

Saida

The demon realm was a place of darkness and strange smells. Plants somehow grew in the rocky ground without sunlight. Many of them glowed eerie shades of blue and purple. Large luminescent insects scuttled away from Malon's wisplight, kept small and dim with the intention of not drawing in any demons.

Saida shivered just thinking about it, and reflexively ran her fingertips across the Crown of Cindra at her belt. The experience of crossing through a demon portal had been . . . unexpected. The one they'd used was deep inside a natural cavern. Malon had taken her hand and led her straight through a wall of dimly glowing green light. She had reached back at the last moment to grab

Brosod. Whatever substance composed the portal seemed to cling to her skin like oil, but once they came out the other side, into this darkness, she was as clean as when she'd gone in. They all were.

Malon stopped walking, holding a small compass near the wisplight. The odd glowing plants reflected their colors on his loose silver hair. "We know north is the general direction we need to go, but you'll have to use your tie to Elmerah for us to find the closest portal."

She glanced over his arm at the compass. She could not even tell north from south in this place. "But the curse is over. I can't sense her anymore. I thought you knew where we were going."

Brosod hopped closer to Saida as a large glowing snake slithered across their path. "Without fresh ingredients, we cannot cast the curse again."

"Keep your voices down," Malon muttered. He handed Saida the compass. "You are a moon priestess. You see things others do not. Use the magic of the circlet and try to find Elmerah."

Saida looked down at the compass in one hand, gripping the circlet still tied to her belt with the other. She tried to focus, but irritation quickly won out. "I don't know how. If I knew we were relying on me to find Elmerah, I never would have agreed to coming down here. I thought you would be able to bring us to the general area of the islands I saw."

"Which is precisely why I didn't tell you. Now you have no choice but to set aside your fears and try."

Brosod sidled a little closer to Saida. "You should try quickly, priestess. My instincts tell me we should not remain in one place for too long."

"She's right," Malon said flatly. "If we wait too long, a greater demon will happen upon us sooner or later."

"You're insufferable," Saida hissed.

She gripped the compass in one hand and the circlet tightly in the other, then closed her eyes. This was just like Malon, tricking her into further exploring the powers of the circlet. *Her* powers. Egrin's words came up in her mind again. Ask him why he agreed to let the Dreilore into Faerune. She pushed the question to the back of her thoughts, focusing on the compass in her hand, and on her need to find Elmerah.

The metal of the circlet turned cold. In her mind's eye, she could see moonlight flowing up through one arm and then down the other, into the compass. Distantly, she sensed Malon and Brosod moving closer, just as she sensed something large and dark not far off, moving toward them.

"We must hurry," Malon whispered.

The compass grew warm in her hand. She heard not a whisper from the circlet, but she knew with sudden surety that the compass would now lead her toward her friend. Had it been Cindra's doing, or her own? She wasn't sure.

"Saida," Malon cautioned, "we need to move."

She opened her eyes, checking that the circlet was

still secure at her belt before removing her hand. "I know which way to go."

"Something is coming near," Brosod whispered, clenching the pole of her spear as her eyes scanned their surroundings.

An unearthly growl trickled from a very large throat.

Malon took Saida's free hand.

"Do we fight or flee?" she rasped.

"Fighting will draw the attention of other demons," Malon explained. "It could greatly impede our progress. I will create a distraction, and we will run."

She felt magic coming from him, then a flash of sunlight lit up the giant creature, much nearer than Saida had realized. Her mind could barely make sense of all of the shiny red limbs, and the huge gaping maw dripping saliva. The creature shrieked, blinded by the sunlight.

Saida stood dumbfounded, blinking stars out of her vision.

"Run!" Malon hissed, already dragging her along.

She ran with her hand still in his, Brosod keeping pace at her other side. The compass pressed against her palm seemed to tug her forward, guiding her in the right direction. Guiding her toward Elmerah.

She realized with a start that it meant Elmerah was still alive. She was still waiting to be found. A demonic shriek, then the clicking of multiple limbs on stone followed after them, and all other thoughts except escape fled from her mind.

CHAPTER FIVE

Saida

Saida ran through a narrow valley amongst strange dead trees, allowing the compass to guide her until it felt like her legs were about to give out. Brosod and Malon ran just behind her, protecting her. They stopped at the base of a rocky cliff, glowing with clinging lichen and vines.

"Up," Malon ordered.

Saida's knees trembled. Neither Brosod nor Malon seemed as winded as her. "You can't possibly be serious," she panted.

"Greater demons are intelligent," Malon explained. "It may still be tracking us. I want the higher ground should it choose to attack."

"I'll help you," Brosod assured.

Saida placed the compass from her sweaty palm into her belt pouch, double-checked the circlet fastened next to it, then wiped her hands on her breeches. "Fine." She gripped a rock just above her head, testing it. The cliff-side seemed secure, and inclined enough to make the climb possible.

Malon and Brosod waited for her to start climbing before they joined her. With her spear strapped to her back along with her bow and quiver, Brosod looked like a hermit crab easily scaling the cliff. A very *dangerous* hermit crab. Panting and sweaty, they climbed onward with darkness stretching endlessly overhead. Saida's hands scraped across rocks and rough vines, her heart pounding so hard she felt faint. One hand reached solid ground above, but she couldn't muster the strength to pull herself up.

It was all she could do to cling to the cliffside while Brosod scrambled past her, then pulled her up. She dragged herself away from the edge, then sat on the rocky dirt, catching her breath.

Malon came up after her, collapsing onto the dirt beside her, breathing heavily. "We should be alright now. If it catches up, at least we'll see it coming. Take a moment to rest, then we'll move on."

Brosod stood over them, bow now at the ready, though her breathing was harsh and her face shone with sweat in the wisplight.

"We've only just begun our journey," Saida's voice trembled, "and we've already nearly been killed. How will we ever make it?"

Malon peered toward the cliff's edge. "I'll admit, I did not expect to run across a greater demon so soon, but we weren't nearly killed. If we had faced it, we would have won, it just would have wasted more time." He pulled around his travel satchel, then offered her a water skin.

She took it, careful not to drink too much, though her body willed her to guzzle the cool liquid down.

She reluctantly offered it to Brosod, who shook her head. "I will only drink when necessary." There was no judgment in her words. She knew Saida had not grown up in the Helshone. She had never learned to survive long periods of time without water.

Saida's racing heart began to slow, but she was quite sure if she tried to stand, her legs would not yet hold her. "Malon," she began, trying to figure out the best way to ask her question. She figured it as good a time as any, for they would not be alone any time soon. As much as she had tried to dismiss Egrin's accusations, they gnawed at her.

Malon took the water skin from her hand and replaced the cap. "Yes?"

The air shifted. A bone chilling shriek deafened her. Her mind barely had time to register the greater demon leaping up from the cliff's edge, its crab-like legs spearing downward toward Malon. She hesitated for just a moment, then grabbed the circlet. Cindra's power flowed through her. For a heartbeat she was pure moonlight, then she sent that power streaming toward the demon. Ice crackled and the demon screamed. Its legs stabbed the ground, trapping Malon.

Saida didn't remember standing, but she had done so at some point as she staggered backwards now. Malon's wisplight winked back into existence, illuminating him trapped within a cage of the creature's many legs, all frozen and fully encased in ice. The creature's huge frozen body, resembling a red beetle but with a humanoid torso, pinned him to the ground.

Brosod stood beside Saida with her bow. She hadn't had a chance to fire a single shot.

Malon cleared his throat. "A little help here?"

Brosod sprung into action, hurrying to tug on one of the creature's frozen legs. It moved with a loud crack, then she tugged on the next until there was enough room for Saida to reach a hand in toward Malon. He took her hand, using the other one to pull himself across the ground until he was free of the creature.

He stood, still holding Saida's trembling hand. "You saved me."

She looked up at him. "You sound surprised," her voice wavered. "It's not like it's the first time."

He smiled, squeezed her hand, then let it drop. "True, but I wouldn't have expected it, then or now."

She turned her gaze away, not wanting him to read

anything in her expression. "We should get moving before we draw anything else."

Malon was quiet for a moment. She could feel him watching her, speculating. "You are right. Lead the way."

Feeling badly shaken, she removed the compass from her belt pouch and started walking. She *had* hesitated. Malon didn't know it, but for just a second, she'd considered not saving him. She had never fully forgiven him for what happened in Faerune, and Egrin's taunting had only brought her worries back to the surface.

She felt the remnants of Cindra's magic still clinging to her. Or was it her magic? They were starting to seem like one and the same. It scared her almost as much as that greater demon. Perhaps more. Because Malon was right, either of them could now best a demon. The thing they needed to be afraid of was themselves. Or more importantly, each other.

Elmerah

E lmerah gnawed on a piece of bread from a loaf she had swiped on their way out of town. She didn't love the idea of stealing, but she was starving, and she would put survival before morals any day. At least to a certain extent. When she had offered Alluin and Killian portions of the bread, neither had accused her of wrongdoing.

Now if she only had silverleaf sap and something alcoholic to ease the pain of her arrow wound. While her burns were a minor annoyance, the deeper wound throbbed like a second heartbeat, making it difficult to breathe.

"I hear voices up ahead," Alluin cautioned from behind her.

She stopped walking, pausing her chewing long enough to listen. Female voices carried on the wind over the sound of bird chatter and small animals darting through the underbrush.

"Some of the elves from the ship," Killian commented, his Nokken hearing even more keen than an elf's.

Elmerah took his word for it, and didn't bother hiding as two elves were revealed coming around a bend in the path. While she didn't particularly care for Vessa, it warmed her heart to see her. After all he had lost, Alluin didn't need to lose his sister too. The second elf at her side, however, Elmerah could have done without.

Vail spotted her, her eyes narrowing, then moving to Alluin as he stepped past Elmerah down the path to meet them.

Killian remained beside Elmerah, his human disguise still in place. "More coming," he whispered. "I smell your sister, she smells a bit like Akkeri."

Her jaw clenched. "Do not accuse her of anything,

she'll only lie. Just keep an eye on her. Let me know if you notice anything else."

Rissine appeared around the bend, spotting Elmerah and Killian beyond the gathered elves. She seemed unharmed, if a little dirty. Zirin came next, favoring one leg.

"Are we going over there?" Killian whispered.

She sighed. "Remember what I told you." She started walking, wondering just what Rissine would have to say for herself. If she even mentioned anything at all.

Alluin turned as she came near. "Vail managed to hold onto some supplies. She can properly tend your wound."

"Wound?" Rissine asked sharply, moving around the elves to look Elmerah up and down. A suspicious glare had Killian losing his disguise.

Elmerah unbuttoned her coat, then tugged one side of her loose blouse over her shoulder.

Rissine stepped closer, observing the bandages.

Elmerah could just barely smell the fishy scent Killian had mentioned. She took a step away from her sister. "Merwyn and Celen are down on the shore. You haven't come across Isara, have you?"

Rissine shook her head. "We saw Celen and Merwyn. A few elves are waiting with them now. As for Isara . . . " She shook her head. "Vessa saw the daft girl run below decks as my ship was sinking. We believe she was trying to rescue her brother." Rissine stepped close again, moving Elmerah's shirt aside before tugging at her bandages.

Elmerah stepped back, out of reach of her sister. "And no one went after her?"

Vail glared at her. "I didn't see you risking your life to save her."

Heat crept across Elmerah's cheeks. "My apologies, I was only skewered by an arrow and half-conscious."

Alluin stepped between them, his attention on her with his back to Vail. "We don't know that she didn't make it out. Let's not jump to conclusions so soon."

He knew her far too well to so quickly reach the heart of her anger. If Isara was gone, no one could neutralize Egrin's magic. Not only that, but the timid sparrow had edged herself into the small group of people that Elmerah called friends.

She nodded once to Alluin, then turned back to her sister. "What do we do now?"

Rissine watched her for a moment. "We find a ship, but first you let the healer tend that wound."

While she had been thinking of it just a moment before, having her sister comment on it made her want to refuse the healing, but she gritted her teeth and nodded. She was feeling spiteful, not stupid.

Vail, however, didn't seem terribly enthused with the prospect. Despite the distaste showing on her lovely features, she hefted a small satchel around her shoulder and stepped toward Elmerah. "You'll need to remove your coat and shirt."

Elmerah rolled her eyes, then nodded toward some trees near the path. She wasn't overly modest, but figured she may as well save Alluin and Killian the embarrassment. Zirin wouldn't care.

She finished unbuttoning her coat as she led the way toward the trees. Once she reached them, she hung her coat from a lower branch, then removed her blouse to reveal her stained underthings. Her wound protested every movement, the bandages stiff with dried blood.

Vail came to stand before her. Even after the ordeal of surviving a sinking ship, she looked well. Her tanned skin seemed to soak up the sunlight. Her rich brown hair had dried perfectly straight and glistening, even after a dip in the salty sea. "It's easier if you sit."

Wincing, Elmerah sat in the grass and leaned her back against the tree.

Vail removed fresh bandages from her satchel, now lightly stained with sea water, and handed them to Elmerah. The bandages were still slightly damp, but better than the ones she currently wore. Vail searched through the rest of her satchel's contents, coming out with a small vial of silverleaf sap. She handed that to Elmerah too, then knelt beside her to start undoing her old bandages.

Elmerah clenched her jaw while Vail went to work, refusing to show how much it hurt.

"You Arthali are a tough lot," Vail commented. "Zirin didn't so much as flinch while I tended his wound, and his is a lot worse than yours."

She took the vial from Elmerah's waiting hand, uncorked it, and started dabbing sap onto the injury. It did little to dull the pain, but it would keep infection from setting in, if it wasn't already too late. Her eyes lingered on a spot closer to Elmerah's collarbone, and she realized the blue mark on her skin was showing. The mark spanned outward with tiny tendrils like forks of lightning. She had incurred it when one of the Fogfaun healed her after she killed a greater demon.

Noticing her gaze, Vail dutifully turned her attention back to Elmerah's wound. "We lost three of our people during the attack. Vessa is telling Alluin now."

She could hear their muttering voices on the path, but hadn't been able to make out the words. Now she was glad she didn't share in the elves' keen hearing. She selfishly didn't want to see how the news would affect Alluin.

"You have brought him much loss," Vail commented.

Elmerah jolted at her words, hissing as Vail's fingers pressed against her wound. "What did you just say to me?" she asked lowly.

"You heard me. If he would have stayed with his people where he belonged, he would not have lost so many."

Elmerah stared at her, but Vail kept her eyes on the wound. "What is your problem with me? We hardly know each other, but I get the feeling you don't like me."

Vail finished dabbing at the sap, then took the bandages from Elmerah's hand. "I'm sure that feeling is mutual. Alluin and Vessa may be willing to trust you witches, but I am not so foolish."

"Then why set sail with Rissine? You could have stayed in Faerune."

Vail pursed her lips as she began bandaging the wound. "The others were going. Vessa talked them into it because she wanted to find her brother. I wanted to find him too, but I also couldn't send them off without a healer. I came to watch over them, and now three of them are lost."

Elmerah turned her eyes forward, not wanting to look at the healer as she asked her next question. "And you blame me? You blame me for their deaths?"

"You, and your sister. You run off on your own because you are powerful enough to survive. Most of us aren't so lucky." She tied off the bandage, but stayed near Elmerah's side. "If you were a true friend to Alluin, you would send him back to his people. You and your sister can see to the emperor yourselves. Alluin has no magic. You don't need him to help you." She stood, gathered her things, and walked back toward the path.

Elmerah stayed seated in the grass for a moment, fury and embarrassment warring within her. Vail was right. They didn't need Alluin to help kill the emperor . . .

But that didn't mean that she didn't *need* him. Was it selfish of her to rely on him so much? To put him in danger when he had no magic?

She knew the answer was yes, but she also knew she

wouldn't try to send him away. Not when he was the only thing holding her together.

Isara

Isara was bone-tired, but she continued walking. At least she had found some seathorn berries to eat along the way. The round orange berries were a bit tart, but with nothing else to eat or drink, she was grateful for them. She popped another one into her mouth as she walked, her hair frothing about her face in the ocean breeze.

After the night of rest, they had decided to return to the shore and walk from there. It was their best chance of finding anyone who might help them.

"You better hope you don't keel over from those berries," Daemon grumbled behind her. "You shouldn't just eat any old thing you find. They could be poisonous."

She ate another berry, savoring the sour juice. "You know, there are benefits to reading books every now and then. Benefits like being able to identify the native plants of different regions."

"My apologies, I've only been busy helping to run an empire."

She glanced back at him. "You speak as if Egrin actually cares for the Empire. I don't believe he does. I think he has only his own goals in mind, and he cares not what you do."

He caught up to walk at her side. His clothing and hair had fully dried by the fire overnight, and his curls now puffed out around his face. "He may be a demon, but he has done a lot for Galterra. The people are happy there."

His words tasted more sour than the berries. While it had been years since she'd visited the Capital, she had not remembered it as a happy place. Sure, the people were protected by high walls and the militia, but there were large gaps in the social classes and crime ran rampant in the slums.

She glanced at her brother, wondering if he had ever even been to the slums. "And you were happy there?"

She didn't miss the flicker of hesitation in his eyes. "Happy enough."

"And you were happy roaming around with Dreilore? Did you ever stop to think that one of those under your command might have been our father's murderer?"

He stopped walking. Placing his hands on his hips, he looked her up and down. "Just what would you like me to say? That I enjoy the company of Dreilore? I assure you, I do not. But they now protect Galterra from the Faerune and Valeroot threat."

She wrinkled her nose. "There is no Faerune and Valeroot threat. There never was."

His cruel smile made her sick to her stomach. "As far as the people of Galterra are concerned, the elves would see the whole city destroyed. While I do not enjoy the Dreilore, they are a necessary part of Egrin's plan."

She crossed her arms, waiting patiently. "Which is?"

He tsked at her. "I think not, dear sister. If your witches are the only way for us to get off this godsforsaken island, then I won't offer you any information to feed to them."

"You've given up on Egrin rescuing you?"

Another flicker of hesitation made her suspect he was hiding more than just Egrin's plans from her. "Well he hasn't come yet," he answered curtly. "And I'm not about to starve waiting for him. As for our father's murderer, Egrin has sworn to me that he'll find out what really happened."

She shook her head and started walking. "You shouldn't pretend to care."

He caught up to her again. "I'm not the one who ran away. Some might think you were the one who didn't care."

She acted without thinking, and only realized what she'd done when her hand was left stinging from colliding with Daemon's face.

He stared at her in shock, rubbing his bright red cheek. "You are most certainly not the sister I remember."

She bit back tears. "No, I am not, and you would do well to not forget it." She clenched her hands into fists and kept walking, unwilling to let him see her cry. Unwilling to let him see the truth.

Because in reality, she was exactly the girl he used to know. Scared to death, and unsure what to do. Completely reliant on others to guide her.

And she knew, deep down, Daemon was the same.

CHAPTER SIX

Elmerah

Elmerah sat across from her sister, slurping her fill of fish stew. It wasn't her favorite dish, flavored heavily with kelp, but she was so hungry she would eat slugs if it came to it. After she cleaned her bowl, she downed her second mug of vibrant wine made from tart berries gathered on the island. While spice and provisions trade with pirates was frequent, the local fare dominated.

Her sister watched her with a scrutinizing eye. She looked tired—older. Elmerah knew it wasn't true, powerful witches aged slowly, but still, her sister seemed different now.

Rissine glanced down at Elmerah's empty bowl, then up to her face. "You know, you *could* say thank you."

She set down her empty mug. "Yes, I *could,* but I won't. Leave it to you to be the only one to hang onto her coin purse on a sinking ship."

Rissine pushed her own empty bowl away with a sour expression.

A few fishermen seated at another table in the small doorless hut gave them occasional glances, but didn't pay them too much mind. In a place like this, people tended to their own business. It was an unwritten code, part of why she had remained so long. Evening was wearing on. Soon the men would finish their suppers and go home to rest.

Rissine crossed her arms beneath her emerald coat and leaned back in her chair. "I'm surprised you didn't offer to help the elves in their search for Isara, given that you used to live here."

Elmerah lowered the finger she had started to lift to summon another mug of wine. "How did you know?"

"Well I did have to find you before I had you kidnapped. Most may pass unnoticed in these parts, but a pureblood Arthali witch will stand out anywhere. Even one living in a pathetic hut far from port."

Elmerah placed her elbows on the table, using her hands to support her chin as she leaned forward. "I didn't offer to help because the elves are the best trackers around, and the Nokken can use his nose. You and I would simply get in the way. We are more useful waiting here to see if Isara shows up."

"And the hot meal and wine had nothing to do with it."

Elmerah rolled her eyes, wondering if she should tell her sister the truth. As soon as discussions had begun, it was clear no one was going to volunteer to wait with Rissine. They all went to look for Isara instead. Even Zirin. Or perhaps he only went because he was Rissine's spy.

Rissine mirrored her position, observing her. "So many thoughts dance through your eyes, sister. Is there something you would like to ask me?"

What were you doing with the High King of the Akkeri? she thought. Out loud, she asked, "Do you think we'll be able to buy passage on a ship back to the mainland?"

Rissine nodded. "It will be a pirate ship, but yes, I have enough to buy us passage. What we will do once we reach the mainland though—"

"You know what we must do," Elmerah interrupted. The plan had never changed. They had only set sail to escape the Dreilore, and to evade the Arthali hunting them.

Rissine glanced around. The fishermen had cleared out, leaving them alone with only the proprietor, who had his back to them as he stirred his large cauldron of fish stew. She leaned closer, pressing her body against the small table. "And just how do you plan on killing a demon when you can't summon even a lick of magic? I didn't track you down just to watch you die. We should return to Faerune."

Rissine's words were like a punch in the gut. "To do what? Keep waiting? Keep watching people die?" She shook her head. "He turned our own people against us. They will track us wherever we go, and if they catch us without Isara, they will kill us."

"Or give us to Egrin," Rissine added. "It does seem he wants us alive, for now."

Elmerah shivered, recalling her time spent with the demon emperor. "He would put us in magic nullifying shackles. Then he would beat us and crush the air from our lungs repeatedly until we were weakened. Once we couldn't fight back, he would do *anything* to find out where our magic comes from. To use it just like he'll use the moonstones he stole from the elves."

Rissine watched her closely, absorbing the information. Elmerah had never shared the specific details of her time in captivity with her sister. "And what do you think he's going to use all of this magic for, once he has it?"

She shrugged. "Nothing good. Demon portals are already popping up everywhere. Maybe he wants to build a new empire. An empire of demons."

"But if he can already open the portals, then why gather magic? It would seem he already has all that he needs."

Elmerah watched her sister, once again wondering about the Akkeri. She had never told Rissine about her experience with the Fogfaun, and what they had told her about Egrin. She decided on the partial truth. "Don't ask me how I came across this information, but as a demon, Egrin comes from a realm of magic. There simply isn't enough magic floating around this land for the taking. It keeps him from achieving his true power. We are both like him, our magic comes from within, but this land is our natural . . . habitat."

Rissine stroked her chin, considering. "Well that explains why he wants the magic, but not what he's going to do with it."

"I don't think any of us will know that until it happens."

"Unless Daemon Saredoth knows," she countered. "You should have let me torture him."

"We would have lost Isara." Not to mention that Elmerah didn't have the stomach for torture. She would kill someone who attacked her, or she would frighten the life out of someone to get answers, but that was different.

"And now they may both be lost to us. So if we cannot return to Faerune, we need a new plan."

Elmerah leaned back in her seat. The proprietor had exited the hut, leaving them in silence save the distant chatter of the docks, and the gentle bubbling of the stewpot. "*We?* You would come with me?"

Rissine wrinkled her nose, scrunching the skin around her dark eyes. "Well I'm not letting you go alone. Especially when you're having . . . *issues* with your magic."

Curse it all, she thought. *I need to know what she was doing with the Akkeri*. "Rissine, Killian saw—"

Shouts from the docks cut her off. Rissine stood and moved to the entrance, peering outward.

Shaking her head, Elmerah joined her, and was quickly filled with elation. A large ship was coming in toward the dock. One large enough to carry them all to the mainland, for a price. The sunset cast rays of pink light across the ship, making it difficult to determine much more than that.

Rissine crossed her arms and narrowed her eyes as the ship neared, its gray sails now distinguishable. *Pirate sails*. "We will go down and see who disembarks. I'll need to come up with a good story to tell them."

"I'll let you handle that part," Elmerah agreed. "You have more experience with *pirates*."

Rissine chuckled. "You won't ever forgive me for sending them after you, will you?"

"I won't ever forgive you for a lot of things," Elmerah muttered, but her sister was already walking out toward the docks.

$$\times$$

Daemon

W*hy me?* was all Daemon could think as they trudged through the cooling sand. He was sure his cheeks were as red as Isara's at this point, burnt by the same sun that now lowered, blinding him with its reflection off the water.

He knew there would be no reprieve from hunger or the ache in his feet any time soon. As far as they walked, they would never reach civilization. Egrin had seen to that. Instead of using his magic on Isara, he had used it on their surroundings, cloaking them so fully with illusion that no one would ever find them.

Bond with her, he had ordered. As if the demon emperor knew anything about bonding.

He probably knew just as much as Daemon, really. He had never been good with relationships, especially those with his sister and father. He was just so unlike either of them. They could never see eye to eye.

He supposed now was the time to learn if he ever wanted to get off of this cursed island. He would have to convince Isara that he knew best. To convince her to stand against the witches rather than Egrin.

He suspected the possibility was the only thing keeping Isara alive. If Egrin couldn't use her, he would have her killed.

As much as Damon resented his family, he couldn't let that happen.

Saida

Despite her hesitance to light a fire, Saida was grateful Malon had convinced her. She huddled close to the flames. Some primal part of her told her that light was safe, darkness was danger. The best path to survival was to light up the darkness.

To light up the darkness, and hope no greater demons came. According to Malon, the lesser would be afraid of the fire.

She watched him out of the corner of her eye sitting next to her, noticing how the flames danced on his iridescent hair. They were supposed to be resting while Brosod took the first shift at standing guard, but neither had made any attempt at sleep.

She glanced over her shoulder at Brosod, standing a few paces away, her back turned as she watched the darkness.

"There is something on your mind," Malon observed.

She turned to find him watching her, his reflective eyes making him look half-blind. "There are many things on my mind. How could there not be?"

He leaned close and lowered his voice. "You were going to ask me something before the greater demon attacked."

She went still. Was she a fool to even ask? She wasn't sure, but she would be a bigger fool to let Egrin manipulate her. "Why did it have to be the Dreilore? Why was letting them into Faerune the only option?"

He turned his gaze toward the fire, as if he found it difficult to meet her eyes while he explained, "For a city to be rebuilt, it must first fall. Nothing would ever change otherwise."

"But the innocent lives—"

"Yes, some were lost, but I convinced much of the guard to abandon the city not to end lives, but to spare them."

"That doesn't make any sense."

Malon sighed. He looked tired. More tired than she had ever seen him. "Egrin's goal was the moonstones. He did not care how many elves lived or died. The Dreilore did not seek out those who hid in their homes. They went straight for the High Temple. They would have accomplished their task no matter what role I played, but in having the guard stand down, lives were spared."

It felt like a fist gripped her heart and was starting to squeeze. "Except my mother."

"She was supposed to be safe, hiding with the rest of the High Council. I've told you that."

She took a few deep breaths, forcing away the pain. She could not think of it now. "You gave our people's magic to a demon. You let the Dreilore in on the assumption that they wouldn't burn the homes with innocents inside."

Finally, he met her eyes. "He would have taken *every-*

thing. By making a deal with him, I was able to make my own plan. I was able to claim the Crown of Arcale."

She pressed her palm against the pain in her chest. "You were able to take it after my mother died protecting it."

He lifted a hand toward her, hesitated, then finally set it upon her shoulder. "If I could have saved her, I would have. I was too late. Elmerah tried her best to avenge her. She saved your father."

"I know," she breathed. "And now she needs me, and I'm stuck in the demon realm."

"We'll reach her soon."

Tears threatened, choking her next words. "I can't lose her too, or my father."

His hand slid across her shoulder. When she didn't move away, he pulled her a little closer. "I won't let you down again."

She felt frozen, and unbearably cold despite the fire. "You can't promise that."

"No, I can't promise that those you care about won't die. I can't promise that either of us will survive this. But I can promise that I won't let you down. In this life, our own actions are all we can control."

She trembled, considering pulling away, but in truth she appreciated the comfort. She had closed herself off so fully after her mother's death, she had never allowed anyone to console her. "I still don't forgive you for what happened to Faerune. You could have warned them. They could have fought."

"They would have died."

She moved her fingers to brush the circlet at her belt. "I'm going to avenge them. I won't let my mother's death be in vain."

"Of that, I have no doubt."

She pulled away enough to see his small smile. While she could not fully accept his answers, she understood. She finally understood why he had done it. But that didn't mean that it was right. And it showed her just how ruthless Malon could be in pursuit of his goals. She wanted to trust him—he had just told her the truth—but his reasoning didn't quite sit right, and that's what Egrin had wanted. He wanted her to fear what Malon might do next. He wanted her to worry about who else might get killed as a result.

Or maybe Malon *had* lied, and Egrin was simply waiting for her to figure out the truth.

Either way, the demon emperor had one thing wrong. Even if she didn't trust Malon. Even if she turned against him, she knew she could never give away the circlets. Her mother had died to keep the Crown of Arcale from Egrin Dinoba, she would sooner die herself then give it to him.

Though her thoughts were a wild tangle, she finally rested, feeling safe in the circle of a traitor's arms. She knew she could no longer be as she once was. She needed to be as ruthless as Malon, and as brave as Elmerah. But just what would that make her? A traitor? An outcast?

It didn't matter what titles she bore, she supposed. It was the price of becoming a leader.

Alluin

Alluin returned to the dark, quiet port, beaten and tired. He would find Elmerah, tell her the news, then return to the camp where everyone else waited. His feet dragged across the dirt path. He only wanted rest, but first he had to face Elmerah's pain and disappointment. They had scoured the entire island, and there was no sign of Isara. Perhaps she had made it to a different island, but in all likelihood, she had gone down with the ship. They had taken her from a peaceful existence and had gotten her killed.

Guilt swam across his skin, coating him like oil. He had helped convince Isara to join them. Her death was on his hands. He had rallied his people to fight, and now more were lost. He brought nothing but ruin to everything he touched.

"Not much of a hunter, are you?" Elmerah's voice came from behind him.

He turned, finding her leaning against a wall in the shadows of a vacant building. He had walked right past her.

"You didn't find her," she observed. "I can read it on your face."

He moved toward her. "We searched the entire island."

She inclined her head, draping her dark hair across her shoulder. "At least now we know for sure. Rissine bought us passage to the mainland."

He leaned against the wall beside her, bone-tired. "We should search one more time in the morning. If we find a smaller boat, we can visit the neighboring islands."

"She never could have swam so far. She's gone."

He fell silent. His heart hurt. Tomorrow they would leave the island, and they would have to admit that those lost were gone forever.

Her bandaged hand brushed his palm, then her fingers laced with his. They stayed silent like that for a long while, a quiet remembrance of all they had lost.

CHAPTER SEVEN

Elmerah

E lmerah could hear the others milling around her, but she couldn't quite bring herself to wake. She listened to the hushed conversations, feeling half in a dream. She had slept with her back in the dirt and leaves, probably further staining her gray coat. She usually chose black for a reason.

Her shoulder wound was a dull throb, aching only slightly more than her burns and the rest of her tired muscles.

"Get up," her sister's voice sounded right above her. "We don't want to miss the ship."

She let out a groan, still not opening her eyes. "I don't

want to deal with pirates today. The last time didn't end well for any of us."

She could clearly picture Rissine standing with her hands on her hips above her, gilded by the early morning light. "Well those nice pirates are our ride back to the mainland, and I'm paying good coin to get us there."

"They'll probably just toss us overboard halfway," she muttered.

"They wouldn't dare."

And she was right. The pirates were mortal men. They would be hard-pressed to toss four Arthali overboard without heavy casualties, and they knew it. It was lucky they had agreed to the transport at all. Lucky that Rissine had offered them a rare rhodium gull for their efforts. Greed was a splendid motivator.

Elmerah finally opened her eyes, staring up at her sister looking down.

Rissine's long black hair draped across either side of her face. Her expression softened. "Best not to think about it," she said, then walked away.

Elmerah didn't ponder long on what she meant. There were too many things she didn't want to think about. She sat up and rubbed her aching head, glancing around their impromptu camp. Most of their supplies had been lost when the ship sank, so there wasn't much to pack up. They would buy what they could at port before their departure. Alluin waited across the clearing, speaking with Vessa and Vail.

Elmerah wrinkled her nose as she glared at the healer's back, remembering her words the day before. *Stupid elf.*

She stood and stretched her uninjured arm over her head. As she lowered it, Celen approached and looped an elbow around the back of her neck. He smelled like sweat and seaweed. "I thought you were going to snore forever."

"I wasn't snoring," she hissed, wincing as his weight strained her wound. She noticed Merwyn and Killian huddled close together, chatting about who knew what. Such an unlikely pair to form a friendship. They all were.

"I will miss the little sparrow," Celen said solemnly.

Elmerah felt her eyes darken. "I don't want to talk about it." She pulled away from his arm and walked toward Alluin and the other elves.

She only made it halfway, then stopped as the tiny hairs at the back of her neck prickled. A familiar sensation chilled her bones.

Rissine was at her side in an instant, drawing her rapier. "Do you feel it?"

Elmerah reached for her cutlass, then cringed when she remembered it wasn't there. She had never been skilled at directing her magic without a weapon, and now she might not be able to summon it at all.

Celen reached her other side. "What are you two suddenly up in arms about?"

"Demons," they said in unison.

Celen was yet to encounter them. He wouldn't recognize the air of unease that accompanied their presence.

Everyone in the camp had stopped talking, all turning to watch Elmerah and Rissine.

"Be ready!" Rissine shouted.

Those still with weapons drew them, and Zirin approached Rissine's other side. Rissine lifted her rapier. Seconds later, thunder answered.

Elmerah's gut clenched at the sound of something large slithering through the grass and brush. Without warning, it reared before them, a creature like a giant centipede with deep purple scales. The camp exploded into motion as more creatures reared up around them.

Rissine's lightning flashed down, striking the nearest demon. Rumbling earth signaled the start of Celen's magic and a demon was swallowed whole into the ground right before Elmerah's eyes.

She staggered back behind Rissine and Celen. She reached for her fire, but nothing answered.

"Fire!" she shouted to Rissine. "They fear fire the most!"

Rissine slashed her rapier through the air, sending flames barreling toward the next demon. The elves had fallen back behind her, fending off the demons who had circled around them.

She heard a grunt of pain, turning toward it just in time to see one of the demons pouncing Celen. Giant pincers clamped down around his arm.

The shrieking demons closed in. There were too

many of them. Elmerah fisted her hands in her hair, squeezing shut her eyes as she tried desperately to summon her magic. They were all going to die.

A trickle of fire built in her heart, quickly swelling to the size of a fist. She opened her eyes just as a demon loomed over her, then her fire exploded outward.

She screamed, trying to reign it back in. She couldn't explode right in the middle of everyone. But there was no stopping it. Her eyes slammed shut as her fire cut across the air all around her. She waited for the screams, but nothing came.

She crumpled to the ground, her heart crying out inside her. *What had she done?* She couldn't open her eyes to look. She didn't want to see. No one could've survived the flames.

Something gripped her arm, then Alluin's voice. "Elmerah. Elmerah it's alright, it's over."

She opened one eye just a crack. Everyone was staring at her like she had just sprouted two extra heads, but they were mostly unharmed. They hadn't been burned alive.

She opened the other eye. The demons had not been so lucky. They were nothing but empty charred exoskeletons.

She looked up at Alluin, unable to stop her tears. "The fire, it didn't touch you?"

Alluin shook his head. She didn't like the haunted look in his eyes. He knelt beside her and gingerly lifted her hand for her to look at. It wasn't as bad as last time.

She hadn't nearly burned the flesh from her bones, but she had burned away the bandages and the sleeves of her coat. She used her free hand to pull her hair forward over her shoulder. Parts of it had gotten even shorter.

Alluin helped her to stand. He looked her over for other signs of damage, but it seemed like it was just her clothes.

Some of the others were pretending not to look now, but Rissine eyed her boldly. "You could have burnt yourself alive."

Pulling away from Alluin, Elmerah lightly brushed flecks of ash from her hands and wrists. "The demons are gone," her voice shook. "Let's get on the ship before more come."

Some of the elves had turned at the sound of approaching footsteps.

Elmerah froze, wondering if more demons approached, then her heart sputtered.

"Saida?" she gasped.

Outlined in the slowly clearing smoke were Saida, Malon, and a female Makali warrior. Elmerah had only seen a few of her race before, but they were easy to recognize. Saida tugged against Malon's grip on her arm.

Unsteady on her feet as she was, Elmerah stormed toward them, her mind not fully registering that perhaps Malon was keeping Saida back from the potential of more fire. All she saw was Malon manhandling her friend.

Saida tugged away from Malon, then stepped in front

of him as Elmerah reached them. She lifted her hands, watching her friend warily. "He's on our side, don't kill him. He was just keeping me back in case there was more fire." Saida glanced around at the fallen demons, then up to her friend. "Did you do this?"

Elmerah let out a harsh bark of laughter. "Yes, and I am so drained now I couldn't kill a fly." She stared at Saida, hardly believing she was real. Yet here she was, dressed in fine yet simple clothes, unharmed. The Crown of Cindra glinted at her belt, and the Crown of Arcale at Malon's. What in Ilthune's name was going on? Elmerah could feel the others watching her, probably thinking she had gone mad, but she didn't care.

Seeing that Elmerah wasn't about to murder Malon, Saida finally lowered her hands. "We were forced to open another demon portal to reach you. Unfortunately, a few other things slipped through before we could cave in the entrance."

Elmerah blinked at her. Her gaze lifted momentarily to Malon, his lips a tight harsh line across his face, not arguing with what Saida had said. Saida had traveled through a demon portal to reach her. She had faced demons with only Malon and one extra warrior.

"You could have been killed," she rasped.

Saida shook her head. "It was worth the risk."

Feeling like she might collapse, she lunged forward and wrapped her arms tightly around her friend. "I missed you," she breathed.

Saida returned the hug fiercely. "I missed you too."

Saida

"I don't like this news about the Akkeri," Malon said.

Saida could barely hear him over the water lapping at the sides of the ship. By the time they had reached the port, word had spread about strange creatures infesting the island, and the pirates were more than ready to depart as soon as supplies were gathered. They hadn't even questioned their strange group of passengers, including Merwyn hunched beneath a cloak.

"They all could have been killed because of me," she sighed.

"*Should* have been killed," Malon countered. He held up a hand at her suddenly rage-filled expression. "I don't mean it like that. But why did the Akkeri not hunt them down? Why stop at sinking their ship?"

She gazed out at the island growing smaller in the distance. She could still smell the smoke from Elmerah's fire on her clothing. "I don't know. I agree, it makes little sense. Hotrath will stop at nothing to reclaim me." She narrowed her eyes at two blond figures walking across the shore. "Is that—" She glanced at Malon, but he was looking in the other direction, out across the sea.

When she looked back, the two figures were gone, but she could have sworn . . .

"What is it?" Malon questioned.

She shook her head. "I must just be tired." She looked further down the ship's railing toward Brosod. "Are you well?" she called above the waves.

The Makali woman looked positively green, but nodded.

Malon leaned near Saida's shoulder. "Only Lukali traders are used to ships. Most of the nomadic Makali have never even seen the sea. But back to the Akkeri—"

She sighed. "I do not know Hotrath's plan any more than you. He is able to sense the Crown of Cindra, but he chose not to hunt me across the Helshone, nor did he try to apprehend me during the time I was in Faerune."

"I won't let him have you," Malon said evenly.

Before she could reply, Alluin approached Saida's other side to lean against the railing. "Elmerah finally went to sleep. I imagine she will be out for a while. Last time . . . " He shook his head. "It takes a lot out of her, using her fire in that way."

"She's dangerous," Malon interrupted. "She could have just as easily burnt you alive."

Alluin glared at him. "You don't know what you're talking about."

Saida gripped the railing tightly. She had only witnessed the edge of Elmerah's fire, but she had fully seen the aftermath. It was almost like what they could do with the circlets, but on a larger scale. How the fire had avoided Elmerah's allies was anyone's guess. She could have easily killed them all.

"It doesn't matter," she decided. "We are together now. It's time to put an end to things."

She wondered if their army of Makali was even necessary. She'd been told about what Elmerah did to the Dreilore. She could decimate Egrin's militia all on her own. Of course, without Isara . . .

She squirmed when she realized Malon was watching her. She still felt a bit embarrassed about the night before, sitting so close to him by the fire.

"Perhaps you should go rest with your friend," he suggested.

Rest sounded nice, though it would not come easily. "I fear if I leave you alone, you will be tossed overboard." She gave Alluin a poignant look.

He lifted his hands in surrender, his brown hair streaming in the breeze on either side of his face. "I admit, I considered it, but I would not act so rashly."

Malon sighed dramatically. "I think the one true threat to my life is currently passed out below deck."

His words managed to make her smile, but it was short-lived. He was right, she needed rest. "Just don't stand so close to the railing once I'm gone."

She cast one final glance toward the island, now just a speck in the distance.

"I'll escort you down," Alluin suggested.

She only nodded. Now that rest was a prospect, her weariness overcame her.

Malon patted her arm, then made his way closer to Brosod.

Saida followed Alluin toward the ladder that led below deck. The pirates they passed dutifully kept their gazes averted.

Once they were below deck, Alluin led her toward the cabin where Elmerah rested, then paused beside the door. "You seem different now. Different from when we last saw you."

She smiled softly. "I apologize for how I acted in Faerune. I didn't know how to cope with my mother's death."

He put a hand on her shoulder. "I understand, but that's not what I mean. You seem older now. Less frightened."

"A trek across the Helshone will do that to a person."

He squeezed her shoulder, then let his hand drop. "You will have to tell me about it sometime." He opened the door and stepped back. "Are you sure we can trust him?" he asked before she could enter the room.

Too many different answers warred within her. She settled on the most practical one. "I cannot tell you who to trust, so you will have to make your own judgment where Malon is concerned."

"But do *you* trust him?"

She thought about all she had been through, from the fall of Faerune, to her kidnapping, to barely escaping death at Urali's hands. She had somehow managed to survive it all. "I don't need to trust him. I have finally learned to trust myself."

Alluin watched her for a moment, then nodded. "In

that case, I promise to make sure no one pushes him overboard." He gestured for her to walk into the dimly lit cabin, then gently shut the door behind her.

Once she was alone with Elmerah's sleeping form, she took the time to just observe her friend. Her singed hair, her freshly bandaged hands, and her stained, charred coat. She realized then that she wasn't the only one who had been pushed to her limit. Elmerah had been pushed to the edge, then off a cliff. Her friend needed her now more than ever.

Elmerah

Half-awake, Elmerah froze when she realized someone was sleeping right beside her. Cracking one eye open, she slowly turned her head toward the other person, then relaxed. Saida's sleeping face was serene in the lantern light.

Elmerah rolled onto her side, propping herself up on one elbow. She watched her sleeping friend, struggling to believe she was real. And she had hardly changed, at least in appearance, save a few light bruises along her jaw that Elmerah sincerely hoped Malon hadn't given her. Something opalescent caught her attention, drawing her eye to the Crown of Cindra looped around Saida's belt. Malon had ordered it stolen from Ivran's cellar, only to return it to Saida's possession. Elmerah couldn't help but wonder what his true aim might be.

Saida's pale eyes opened. "You know, it's odd to watch people while they're sleeping."

Elmerah gave her a rueful smile and shook her head. "What happened, Saida? What changed your mind about Malon? He kidnapped you, and now you travel with him willingly? You expect us to share our plans with him?"

Saida lifted one hand to rub her eyes. "I told you about the Helshone, and the Makali."

Elmerah stared her down. "You know what I mean. You blamed Malon for your mother's death. You wanted him to pay for it. Now you are allies? Perhaps something more?"

Saida rolled onto her stomach, bracing her elbows on the sleeping mat to hold up her head. Elmerah realized she had moved a second mat right next to hers. "He thought my mother would be safe with the rest of the High Council. He was a guardsman, he knew about the secret chambers where they were supposed to hide, and he didn't tell the Dreilore about them."

Elmerah sat up, her sore limbs protesting the movement. "But he still let them into the city."

"They would have come regardless."

She watched her friend closely, hardly believing her words. "Are you just repeating what he told you?"

Saida squirmed, looking down at the mat beneath her. "Perhaps, but that does not make it any less true."

"His actions led to your mother being killed," she reiterated.

Saida abruptly turned over and sat up. "You blame Rissine for your mother's death, yet here you both are."

Elmerah frowned. "That does not mean I have forgiven her. It seems like you have forgiven Malon."

Saida hunched her shoulders, peering down at her lap. "I have not decided that yet. Not for sure. But a lot of things happened in the desert."

Elmerah waited for her to continue, wondering what could've possibly happened to change Saida's mind so completely.

"Will you tell me about it?" Saida asked softly. "About what happened with your mother? Why you believe it to be Rissine's fault?"

Elmerah's gut clenched at the thought of answering the question. She took a moment to consider her next words. It was time. She knew it was time, but it didn't make it any easier.

She took a deep breath. "Very well. As you know, my mother was killed by my people." Even just saying the words out loud made her panic, made her want to run away. "Rissine thinks I don't understand that she was just trying to protect me that day," she forced herself to continue. "The other clans had agreed to eliminate Shadowmarsh witches, just to save their own necks. They might have been cowards, but they were still just people like you and I. They wanted to survive, but they didn't want to kill children."

She looped her hands around her knees and looked down at her bare feet, then continued, "Rissine was older, so she was the one they told. They told her our mother would die, and there was nothing she could do about it. I think my mother knew too. I think she asked Rissine to watch over me and keep me safe. Rissine agreed. She took me fishing that day, and we stayed away until nightfall. When we returned, my mother was dead. At the time, I thought Rissine was just as shocked as I. But she lied to me, she knew what was going to happen and she didn't warn me. She didn't let me make my own choice."

Saida's jaw hung slightly agape. "You were both basically children. How difficult must it have been for Rissine to be placed in such a situation? Not strong enough to save her mother, but doing the only thing she could to keep her sister from dying too."

Elmerah hunched forward further, pressing her chin to her knees. "Now you know why I don't share my story. I expected your reaction, but I cannot forgive Rissine. If I knew my mother was going to be killed, I would have fought."

"And perhaps your mother was well aware of that, and that's why she didn't tell you. She wanted to protect you, and Rissine."

Elmerah gripped her calves with her burned hands, squeezing until it hurt. "I should have had a choice."

"You would have chosen to die."

Elmerah's chest swelled with anger, not just at Saida,

but the anger she had been holding onto her entire life. "And what would you have done if you knew in advance that your mother would be killed? If you had been well enough to go into Faerune that day to face the Dreilore, what would you have done?"

Saida was silent for long enough that Elmerah finally looked at her. The young elven priestess sighed. "I would have thrown myself into the Dreilore's path. And I would have hated anyone who got in my way."

"Malon got in your way."

Saida shook her head. "He didn't know that my mother would die. He thought she would be safe. He dosed me with bloodflower extraction to protect me."

Elmerah shrugged. "Or so he says."

"What do you want?" Saida snapped. "Why are you pressing this?"

Elmerah watched her friend. Saida obviously didn't realize the way she looked at Malon. Lust, love, whatever it was . . . it was foolish. And it was blinding her to the truth, whatever the truth might actually be.

"I just want you to be careful," she explained. "You have allied yourself with him, and I will respect your judgment, but please just remember that he did many things against your will."

Saida was silent for a long moment, then nodded. "I will think upon what you have said, but for now, it changes nothing. Together Malon and I can use the circlets. Egrin fears them. I believe we have the power to defeat him."

"And what of your army of Makali?" Elmerah asked.

"They march toward the Capital. Egrin has the Dreilore and the militia to protect him. His armies are greater than ours, but with the circlets . . . and with you and Rissine . . . " her voice cracked with emotion.

Elmerah reached over and took her hand. "We're going to make him pay for all he has done."

There was a fierceness to Saida's eyes that Elmerah had never seen before—a certain measure of defiance that she also recognized in herself. As much as she detested Malon, she had to admit, whatever he had done to Saida had made her strong.

CHAPTER EIGHT

Alluin

Alluin watched the sun slowly setting, its vibrant colors reflecting off the calm sea. Two tense days had passed without incident. He was relieved to see Elmerah's wounds slowly healing, and her energy returning. It seemed with Saida's arrival, a great weight had been lifted off her shoulders. And yet, there was a new tension there, and he wasn't sure what it was about.

Then there was Saida, always speaking closely with Malon or the Makali warrior, Brosod. Alluin was sorely regretting his promise to not push Malon overboard. The elf had lied to and manipulated them all. How could they even begin to trust him with their plan?

His mind heavy with worries, he leaned against the

railing and watched the sea passing by. According to the pirates, they would arrive at a small port the next evening, just north of Aeluvaria. The port was in a hidden cove, unknown to the militia. From there, they had agreed to find the army of Makali. The Makali would have had five days to travel north from Fallshire. Not enough time to reach the Capital, but if they had walked for the entirety of every day, as Malon claimed they would do, they would not be too far off. A few more days for them to reach the woods east of Aeluvaria, then several more after that to reach the Capital.

He sensed someone behind him and turned.

Vail approached. She had tied her sleek brown hair at the nape of her neck. The tail crept over her shoulder, falling nearly to the waist of her simple green tunic. "I thought I would find you up here," she said as she reached him. She joined him near the railing as he turned to look back out across the sea.

"Will we really march with the Makali?" she asked.

You will, he thought. He trusted Vail, but it was safer for everyone if few knew their true plan. "We have been hoping for an army all along. Faerune may have failed us, but according to Saida, the Makali will not."

"But their land is the Helshone, far from the Capital," Vail pressed. "Why would they fight for us?"

In truth, he wasn't quite sure. He had heard the tale, that Saida could bring water and life to the desert, but he found it difficult to believe. No one had that sort of power. "They believe Saida and Malon can wield the power of the gods. They want that power directed toward their homeland. Marching on the Capital is a small cost for what they hope to gain—what they believe Malon and Saida can do."

He glanced over as Vail lifted one highly arched brow. "And what do you believe?"

He shrugged. "I believe Saida speaks the truth. They can wield the power of the circlets. Whether that power comes from the gods, and whether it can bring life to the desert, who can truly say?"

Vail moved closer to him, pressing her shoulder against his. Even after days out at sea, she smelled like the forest. She smelled like home. "I think we should return to Faerune and let the others fight this war. What good will you and I do? What good will Vessa do?"

"You are free to go if you wish. In fact, I would prefer it. And take my sister with you."

He could sense Vail watching him out of the corner of her eye, though she pretended to look out toward the sea. "She will not go without you, and neither will I. But you could come with us."

"I started this thing with Elmerah and Saida. I intend to see it through."

"You owe them nothing. We are your people. You belong with us."

He turned toward her, his skin prickling with sudden anger. "Egrin took everything from us. He slaughtered our people. He turned the Empire against us, and against

Faerune. I will not ask of Elmerah and Saida anything I am not willing to do myself."

"Your nobility will get you killed," she hissed.

"So be it. I will not abandon her—them."

"I think you're in love with that witch," Vail accused. "I think that's the true reason you won't abandon her."

He would have been angry at her tone, but he could sense the pain beneath her words. The loss of a life that could have been, but never would. "My feelings toward Elmerah are my business, not yours. And any choice you make once we dock should have nothing to do with me."

"She's going to get you killed."

He sighed, glancing over his shoulder to where he knew Elmerah was standing with Celen. Her eyes drifted from Celen to meet his waiting gaze. She hesitated on Vail at his side, then looked away.

He turned back to Vail. "She's been saving me since the day she met me. If I die now, that will have been enough."

Vail shook her head. "You're a fool." She pushed away from the railing, then headed toward the ladder that would take her below deck. The pirates milling about paid her no mind. They had all gotten used to each other over the course of the journey.

Alluin turned his attention back to Elmerah, meeting her eyes once more across the deck. He let Vail's words sink in. Truly, he'd had little time to consider his feelings for Elmerah, and he was quite sure she viewed him only as a friend. That was enough for him. If they were to die facing Egrin, then they would go down together. It had been their silent bargain from the start.

Saida

Saida sat in a cabin with Brosod below deck. They would have to act quickly, before anyone else came down to rest. All of the women in the party crammed into the cabin at night. There wasn't enough room on the ship for anything else.

Brosod held a dagger in her hand, looking worried. "Are you sure about this? Perhaps we should consult with Malon—"

"He cannot know," Saida cut her off. "I'll be fine."

"The curse is far more dangerous when you use your own blood to power it."

Saida gripped the Crown of Cindra in one hand. "I trust the goddess to guide me. She has gotten me this far."

Brosod's hand tightened around the hilt of the dagger. "If you cannot be swayed, then we must act quickly before anyone happens upon us. Having someone try to pull you out can be just as dangerous as you going in without proper ritual."

Saida held out her arm, baring her wrist. "I understand the risks."

Brosod took Saida's hand, moving it so her forearm was poised above a beeswax candle burning between them. "Remember everything I have told you."

Saida closed her eyes. "I remember. Do it."

She winced as the blade sliced across her inner forearm. Hot blood dripped down her skin, then hit the candle flame, sizzling with every drop. Brosod began to chant.

Still gripping the circlet in her free hand, Saida chanted with her. More blood sizzled onto the candle, then Brosod helped Saida lean back upon her sleeping mat. Once the curse took hold, Brosod would pretend to sleep too, but she would be there in case anyone tried to interrupt the curse.

Saida's thoughts drifted, then slipped away entirely. The sleeping mat beneath her faded from her senses as darkness consumed her. It was easier this time, stepping into the dream realm. Only this time she wasn't searching for any of her friends. She was searching for a demon.

She had taken but a few steps across the hard stone when he found her. "Have you reconsidered my offer?"

She turned to face him. He looked just the same as when she last saw him in his black clothing with gold and silver embroidery. His short black hair was so sleek it looked almost like the feathers of a raven. "I want to know why you urged me to ask that question of Malon. Did you think his answer would turn me against him?"

Egrin's smile was more a baring of teeth. "Yes, if he actually told you the truth."

She crossed her arms, feigning indifference. "And what is the truth?"

He took a step toward her, and it was a struggle to not run away. "The truth, little elf, is that I did not approach him with an impossible bargain. He came to me. His spies believed I would soon move against Faerune, and they were right. He came to me and offered to help."

Her gut twisted. "I don't believe you. You would have come for the moonstones one way or another."

Egrin strolled closer. "In that, you are correct. But I already had Nokken within Faerune. Their task was simple. Poison the High Council. Pose as healers so they would be close when each member died. Hide the bodies, then impersonate the council members long enough to infiltrate the High Temple and steal the moonstones. I could have had what I wanted without lifting a finger."

She abruptly realized he had moved so close she could feel his breath. She staggered back like he had struck her.

He quickly closed the distance between them once again, stalking her like a predator. "So you see, I was all set. Then an elven guardsman sent word to me. He had some very interesting things to say, and requested a meeting. He convinced me he knew the location of the Crown of Cindra, which had been missing for countless decades. If I went about things his way, he would tell me the location of both the circlets."

Saida didn't try to move away again. She stood completely enthralled by his tale. Could it be the truth?

"You see," he went on, leaning close. "A bargain with one of my kind is completely binding. I was too prideful to see that the guardsmen was tricking me in the same way I tricked the High King of the Akkeri. I told Hotrath I would obtain a moon priestess. There were no terms put in place to ensure a safe delivery. Malon told me he would divulge the location of the circlets, but not that he would give them to me. I didn't think I would *need* him to give them to me. I only needed to know where they were. He used me to tear down Faerune, then he fled with the Crown of Arcale. Once I finally located him, he had you, and both the circlets."

She clutched her stomach, feeling ill as she absorbed his words. Egrin had intended the deaths of the High Council, but he had not intended to waste the time directly assaulting Faerune. Malon had brought that about himself.

Egrin smiled. "I'm told your mother died that day. Orius was quite proud to claim the kill."

Her mouth went dry. *Orius.* Her mother's murderer now had a name.

"I could give him to you," he went on. "In exchange

for the circlets, and Malon's death." He tilted his head like a bird. "And of course, Faerune will be safe."

Tears choked her throat. She couldn't seem to form a reply.

His smile broadened. "Think about it. You still have a little bit of time before the full moon, but don't think for too long. Once the moon reaches its apex, I will obliterate Faerune so completely it will be as if it never existed."

He snapped his fingers and disappeared, leaving her alone in the near darkness.

Tears fell down her cheeks. She really was alone. Not just here, but on the ship.

It was her choice to make. She could save Faerune and have her mother's murderer put to death. But if she took Egrin's offer, would she doom them all?

Isara

"Can't you work any faster?" Daemon asked, crossing his arms to lean against a wooden post at the docks. The moon and stars were mostly shrouded by clouds, hiding his haughty features.

Isara tossed a string of fish guts into a nearby bucket. "You know, it would go a lot faster if you helped. We would have already had a nice supper by now if I weren't doing all the work myself."

Daemon lifted his hands and wiggled his fingers. "These hands do not touch blood and guts."

With a heavy sigh, Isara retrieved the next fish and began cleaning it. They had happened upon the small port the day before, though she could have sworn they'd already searched this area of the island. It was like the port had appeared out of thin air, or else a veil had been lifted.

Since they had no coin, she had made a bargain with a fisherman. They would do some extra work, and in exchange would receive a hot meal and a place to stay for the night. Perhaps if they waited in the port long enough, Elmerah and the others would find them.

Although . . . she wasn't sure how they had managed to miss each other for this long on such a small island. Maybe she and Daemon were the only ones to survive the sinking ship. Or else the others had ended up on another island entirely.

She tossed another string of guts into the bucket, unfazed by the blood and slime on her fingers. "Perhaps we can find enough work to earn passage to the mainland."

She was surprised when he moved forward and sat beside her, dangling his legs off the edge of the dock. "Or maybe we should just stay on this island. Let the witches and Egrin have it out, and we'll remain here where it's safe."

She eyed him suspiciously. "So you've given up on him finding you?"

Daemon shrugged. "It's been days. I fear it's just you and I now, dear sister."

She continued to watch him, her hand halfway toward grabbing the next fish. "You don't seem terribly upset about that."

He peered out across the dark water. His once fine clothing was stained and torn, and his hair was a fluffy mess. At least his arrow wound was healing nicely. "I'll admit, it hasn't been utterly awful spending this time with you, and away from Egrin. You must at least feel *some* relief to be away from those crude witches."

He was wrong. She didn't feel relief, but . . . where had they gone? Had they abandoned her?

Daemon surprised her even further by reaching across her lap to grab a fish from the brimming basket. He lifted one of the knives the fisherman had given them, but couldn't seem to decide where to poke it through the scales. Finally, Isara picked up another fish and began to instruct him.

He listened, and before long they had a nice hot meal in a fisherman's hut. Then they went to sleep on stiff mats, but with warm blankets.

She couldn't help but think, as she drifted off to sleep, how nice it would be to live a different life with her brother, far from witches, elves, and demons. Far from anything else that could bring her any more pain.

CHAPTER NINE

Alluin

On the evening of the following night, they finally reached shore. The rocky cliffs of the hidden cove loomed around them like silent sentinels, guiding the ship toward the torches burning at the small pirate-built dock. Alluin could see a few shadowy figures waiting by the torches, and couldn't help but wonder if this was where the pirates would turn against them. Dread settled into his stomach. Perhaps a rhodium gull was not enough motivation after all. Not when you had two witches with bounties on their heads. The pirates could keep the gull and sell Elmerah and Rissine to the emperor. Of course, they'd have to capture them first, and would surely suffer many casualties.

Elmerah and Saida moved to stand with him as the ship reached the dock. Saida had a satchel of supplies, the Crown of Cindra, and a dagger at her belt. Elmerah had nothing but the coat on her back, and even that was coming apart at the sleeves where her magic had burned the fabric.

Alluin glanced over his shoulder to see Brosod and Malon standing nearby. Neither ever let Saida long out of their sight. Brosod, he believed, genuinely cared for Saida's safety. Malon . . . he should have pushed overboard while he had the chance.

The men on shore began roping the ship to the dock while those on board set to carrying up whatever cargo they were smuggling from below deck.

"Let's go," Elmerah said. "I'm ready to be on dry land."

Saida watched Elmerah go with a strange expression. Neither woman had mentioned what happened between them the first night on the ship, but that odd tension was still there.

Malon and Brosod walked past and Saida joined them, patting Alluin's arm as she walked away. He wondered if they had figured out the plan. The plan that he, Elmerah, and Celen had kept to all along. Killian was still involved too, mostly because he had known about it from the start and didn't believe that any of them would be swayed from their course.

Celen came up behind him and leaned an elbow on his shoulder. "Not far from the Capital now, are you having second thoughts?"

Alluin shook his head. "No, but keep your voice down." He walked out from under Celen's elbow toward the wide plank that now bridged the ship and the dock. He walked down after Vessa and Vail, both being quiet and not acknowledging him.

The other elves in their party came down next. He guiltily realized he had never even learned their names. They were from one of the southern Valeroot clans, brave men who had volunteered to accompany Rissine on her mission. And they had been treated as little more than pawns—disposable.

He reached the dock, then followed the others down the planks toward the shoreline, silently vowing that if they survived, he would learn everyone's names. He would make sure they were rewarded the recognition they deserved. But for now . . . there was no time to get to know them. At the first opportunity, he and the others would branch off from their group and head straight toward the Capital.

Feeling weary and morose as he reached the sand, he waited alone. Several large crates had already been carried down to dry land. The men on shore were moving them toward rough wagons with large, wide wheels, capable of being pulled by horses across sandy or bumpy terrain.

Rissine and Zirin both spoke with the captain, watching from the dock as his men unloaded their goods. Coin was exchanged, then Rissine and Zirin moved toward the rest of their group gathering further off shore.

Once more uneasy, Alluin joined them.

Rissine addressed the group. "The pirates say strange creatures now roam the land, some doing the bidding of the Dreilore, if these men are to be believed . . . "

Alluin's arms prickled at her words. That was it then, the feeling of dread. It wasn't his intuition telling him the pirates would turn on them, it was the demons. It was as if the land itself had turned dark and foreboding.

Elmerah moved to his side, rubbing her arms beneath her coat. "I don't like this," she muttered.

"I don't like not knowing what Egrin is planning. And I don't like not having a weapon."

"We'll find you something," he whispered, though he wasn't sure how.

"We should get moving," Rissine was saying. "We'll find a safe place to make camp for the night." Finished with her short speech, she moved toward Alluin and Elmerah with Zirin at her heels. She extended a hand back toward Zirin, and he handed her a sheathed cutlass, which she offered to Elmerah. "Lucky for you, the pirates are smuggling weapons."

Elmerah took the cutlass, sliding it partway out of its leather sheath. "Well it's not elven silver steel, but it will work."

Rissine rolled her eyes, the expression exaggerated by the torchlight casting harsh shadows on her lower features. "*You're welcome*, now let's get going." She turned and started walking.

"Alluin could use a new bow!" Elmerah called after her.

"I'm not made of coin!" Rissine called back.

With an apologetic shrug to Alluin, Elmerah walked after her sister. The others formed a line behind and around them as they ventured away from shore, leaving the pirates to finish unloading their smuggled weapons.

"Glad to be rid of those witches," one man muttered in passing.

Elmerah ignored him.

As they moved farther from the shore, Alluin's sense of unease only grew. He wasn't sure if he was actually sensing the demons in the land, or if he was just wary of being so near the Capital. Or perhaps he was just dreading venturing off on their own, going through with their plan to assassinate the emperor . . . without Isara. They would have to kill him before he could even think to react and steal the air from their lungs. It was a long shot, but it was all that they had. Better than trusting Malon to not turn on them when the moment came.

As if summoned by the thought, Saida fell back to walk at Elmerah's other side. "Malon can sense a demon portal near here. We should be wary of where we decide to make camp."

"He probably tore the portal open himself," Elmerah replied sourly.

Saida stared at her, hardly watching her own footing.

"I apologize," Elmerah muttered. "I can feel the dark magic. It makes me uneasy."

"Me too," Saida agreed. "I hope to never travel through another portal."

"Does he know which direction the portal is in?" Alluin asked, hoping to cut the tension. "We should veer away now. It's not wise to travel far at night."

Saida withdrew something from her belt pouch. It took Alluin a moment to realize it was a small compass.

She peered down at it, then pointed to her right. "The demon portal is that way."

"The compass told you that?" Elmerah asked.

Saida put the compass back in her pouch. "I used it to locate you. Now it shows me whatever I want to find. I believe it is the blessing of Cindra."

Elmerah didn't comment, but Alluin knew just what she was thinking. Was it really the blessing of Cindra? Or a trick provided by Malon.

Brosod fell back to walk at Saida's other side. The silence stretched on. Alluin wondered at what point things had started to go so very wrong.

Elmerah

U nable to sleep, Elmerah found herself at the fire late at night with Brosod. Zirin and Vessa stood watch out in the darkness.

Brosod leaned her elbows on her knees, occasionally glancing away from the fire toward Elmerah.

Having had enough of the silence, Elmerah caught her eye the next time she looked. "Is there something you would like to ask?"

Brosod straightened, then nodded. "Yes. Or no. Rather, something I would like to say."

Surprised, Elmerah nodded for her to go ahead.

"Saida went through much to find you, and you do not seem grateful."

Elmerah's eyebrows shot up. "You're rather blunt, aren't you?"

"I speak the truth."

She debated what to say in reply. Brosod was clearly loyal to both Saida and Malon. How could she explain that she was worried Malon was tricking them all, and that Saida would be hurt in the process?

She supposed if the Makali could be so bluntly truthful, so could she. "Malon lied to Saida from the start. Then he summoned demons in order to distract me while he kidnapped her and dragged her across the Helshone. I was hacking apart spider limbs when I saw him carrying her unconscious body away from me. Can you see why I would not be supportive of their alliance?"

Brosod hesitated. Her lips parted as she blinked her

long lashes. "But they are chosen by the gods. None of that matters in the face of something so great."

Elmerah flicked a twig she'd been playing with into the fire. "And is it right for the gods' chosen vessels to travel through demon portals? To summon demons?"

"All of it was done to overthrow the demon emperor, and to save *you*."

She didn't argue that she didn't actually need the saving. With Brosod speaking so freely, there was something else she wanted information on. "Can anyone travel through a demon portal?"

Brosod shrugged. "Malon pulled Saida through, and she pulled me through. I did not think to ask questions beyond that."

Elmerah thought of the one demon portal she had seen. At the time, she had been too busy fighting for her life to test it, but could she have walked through? Could she have used it to travel great distances quickly? "And how did you find your way through once you were there?"

"Malon gifted Saida a compass. She used the magic of the circlet to enchant it. It led her to you." Brosod's back stiffened.

A heartbeat later, Elmerah realized why. Malon stepped forward out of the darkness, his eyes on the Makali. "I'd like a moment alone with Elmerah, if you don't mind."

Brosod hopped to her feet, then scurried away.

Elmerah wrinkled her nose. "She pays far too much heed to your orders."

Malon took Brosod's vacated seat on the ground. "She wants to see her homeland brought to life."

She tossed another dry twig into the fire, watching the small flash of flame its clinging leaves created. "And will you keep that promise? It seems to me you're prone to breaking them."

"The only promise I have made is to protect Saida, and I have done just that."

Elmerah scowled. "If you call manipulation protection, then I suppose that's true."

"You witches are absolutely impossible."

"Then why come for us? Why not convince Saida otherwise?"

His reflective eyes glinted in the moonlight, making it difficult to read his expression. "Saida has helped me a great deal. She has saved my life on more than one occasion. I would not deny her any of her desires, no matter how foolish."

Elmerah snorted at the subtle jab. "We are the only ones gathered around this fire. Spare me the noble martyr act."

He swiped a palm across his face and shook his head. "Why Saida cares about you, I will never understand. But since she does, I will grant you a word of advice."

She flicked another twig, another small burst of flame. "I don't need your advice."

"You won't make it if you try to travel through a

demon portal. If you try, Egrin will find you, and there, he will be at his full power."

"I said I don't need your advice," she hissed. Just how long had he been listening to her conversation with Brosod? "And you went through. Why didn't Egrin come for you?"

"He fears the circlets. Far more than he fears your magic." He hesitated. "And it takes demon blood to travel through a portal. You may not have any."

She paused halfway toward flicking another twig into the fire. She straightened her spine, then looked directly at him. "Are you saying Saida has demon blood?"

"No, I'm saying I have demon blood. Only a trace, but it is enough. I pulled Saida and Brosod through. Perhaps you have demon blood too, or one of the others. It's more common than you think, but it's still a bad idea to go through the portal."

She continued to stare at him. He looked like a pure-blooded Faerune elf to her.

"What is it?" he asked.

She shook her head. "I am just surprised you would actually admit all of this to me."

He turned toward the fire, leaning his elbows on his knees. "Saida already knows, and her opinion is the only one I care about. Honestly, I'm surprised you hadn't already figured it out. You know I can summon demons. You know that Isara is human, but has demon blood too. Egrin is not the only greater demon to ever come through a portal. Their blood is mixed throughout the land."

She twirled the twig in her fingers, considering his words. "So if I even had a little bit of demon blood, I could go through a portal too?"

"Yes, and you would die. Here, Egrin fears your magic. In the demon realm, he would be far more powerful than you. It was a risk even traveling with the circlets, but Saida was insistent."

"He doesn't fear my magic in any realm. He could steal the air from my lungs with a thought."

He leaned one hand back in the dirt as he looked at her, draping silver hair over his shoulder. "Isara has been missing for days. If he didn't fear your magic, he would have taken you before Saida and I found you." He straightened, turning to fully face her. "If you try to run off through a demon portal, you'll die. And your death will hurt Saida. She may become so broken that she will not be up to fulfilling our task."

She rolled her eyes. "You keep assuming that I plan to travel through a demon portal. I was only curious." Never mind that it was exactly what she had been considering. Egrin wouldn't expect it, and she might be able to get the jump on him.

"Have you noticed the small silver whistle your sister wears around her neck?" he asked.

Her anger flared at the sudden mention of her sister. "What does that have to do with demon portals?"

"Everything, if you plan on taking your sister with you."

She clenched her fists. The fire near their boots seemed to burn a little brighter. "What do you mean?"

He glanced around, then leaned in close, meeting her waiting gaze. "Merwyn recognized it, and he confided in Saida. Like Brosod, the tiny Akkeri follows the will of the gods. The whistle was a gift from Hotrath. He can hear its call from any distance."

A chill ran through her, and the fire died down. She wanted to believe he was a liar, but Killian had seen Rissine with the Akkeri. "And what will he do if he hears that call?"

Malon shrugged and leaned away. "I do not know your sister's bargain with the High King, but you should stop wasting your time worrying about me, and worry more about her."

She took shallow breaths. She knew it was a possibility that Rissine would betray her again, but she didn't want to believe it. Not after everything they'd been through. "Hotrath wants Saida. The deal must have something to do with her."

Malon glanced around again, then nodded. "My army is not far. All I ask is that you give us a few days before you go after Egrin. With your magic, the circlets, and my army, nothing will stand in our path. Don't get yourself or Alluin killed with your foolishness, and don't give Rissine a chance to betray us all."

He stood and retreated before she could answer

either way. It was just as well, because she had no idea what her answer might be. Rissine had betrayed her before, and now she had made an unknown bargain with the Akkeri. But Malon had betrayed her too. He had let the Dreilore into Faerune, and he kidnapped Saida.

She knew she could trust Alluin and Celen, perhaps even Killian, and the list ended there. She stood, casting one final glance at the fire. It had died down to almost embers. With a thought, she brought it roaring back to life, then shivered. Her magic was back, and if Malon was to be believed, Egrin feared it. She needed to figure out what to do with that fear before her sister blew her little whistle, and before Malon's Makali arrived. She simply wasn't in the habit of letting anyone—even her own sister—fool her twice.

CHAPTER TEN

Saida

S aida woke the next morning to find their group had greatly decreased in size. All of the Arthali were missing, including Elmerah. Killian and Alluin were gone too.

Brosod returned to where Malon and Saida waited near the remaining embers of the fire. Her dark features were grim. "I tracked them to the edge of camp, then their footsteps simply disappear." Brosod shook her head. "I do not understand it."

Vessa leaned against a nearby tree, her arms crossed. Her shaggy hair shaded her features from the morning sun. "I told you they wouldn't be found so easily."

"And what do you know about it?" Malon asked.

Vessa glanced at the remaining Valeroot elves, then back to Malon. "My brother said as much. He said don't even bother looking."

Malon started toward her, but Saida grabbed his arm to stop him. "Being angry with her will make no difference. Elmerah and the others chose to go." Her throat tightened, choking off anything else she might have said. Perhaps if she had been more open to Elmerah's worries, she wouldn't have left. Had Malon's presence chased her away?

Malon patted Saida's hand, then stepped back, turning his attention to Merwyn, who huddled in the shadows of a large crag. "Did they tell you they were leaving too?"

Merwyn tugged his hood a little further over his face, then shook his head. Covered up as he was, he appeared like a child. He was always so quiet, sometimes Saida forgot he was there. "No." He looked at Saida like he dearly wanted to tell her something, but his crooked mouth simply could not form the words.

She stepped away from Malon and approached the Akkeri, lowering her voice as she reached him. "What is it?" It was difficult to not react to his fishy smell, just another facet of the Akkeri's alleged curse.

Merwyn's chin drooped. "Does Elmerah know—about the whistle?"

Saida's eyes went wide. She had nearly forgotten about Rissine's little whistle. Merwyn had recognized it and confided in her, and she had informed Malon. "I did not tell her. Elmerah and her sister already have issues. I didn't want to jump to any conclusions before we knew the truth. Do you think that's why they left?"

Malon sighed heavily at her back "I told her last night."

Saida whirled on him, her heart suddenly racing.

"I didn't think—I just wanted her to be wary, I didn't think she would take her sister and leave."

She stepped closer, searching his silver eyes for answers. "I don't understand. When did you speak with Elmerah?"

Malon chewed his lip. "I caught her asking Brosod about demon portals. I was afraid she would run away because she doesn't trust me. I wanted to let her know she couldn't trust her sister either. I thought I was doing the right thing."

"Now wait just a—" Vessa interrupted, pushing away from her tree.

Malon held up a hand to cut her off, his attention still on Saida. "Elmerah believed that any deal Rissine might make with the Akkeri would concern you, but she also believes she needs her sister's help to defeat Egrin."

"So?" she pressed.

Malon rolled his eyes. "In leaving, she keeps Rissine at her side, but away from you. I believe that is why she has gone. I swear, if I had known this would be the result, I wouldn't have told her."

Saida opened her mouth, then shut it as she processed his words. She shook her head. "I should have been the one to tell her about the whistle. I should have told her the moment we found out. Elmerah didn't trust me enough to come to me about it before leaving."

Malon moved toward her, placing his hands on her shoulders. "It's me she doesn't trust. She left because she's trying to protect you from her sister."

She raised her chin, sealing her emotions away to deal with later. "So what do we do now?"

"We continue as planned. We find our army, and we march on the Capital. If the gods are truly with us, we will arrive in time to aid Elmerah." He glanced over his shoulder at Vessa and the other waiting elves. "You five are free to do as you wish. Return to Faerune if that is your choice."

Vessa shook her head. "Oh no, we aren't going anywhere. Without us, you won't have anyone to show you the way into the Capital. That's the only reason we stayed behind instead of going with my brother. He wanted us to show you."

Malon let his hands drop from Saida's shoulders as he turned to fully face the other elves. "What do you mean?"

Vessa grinned. "I spent most of my life in the Capital. I know the city like the back of my hand. I also know all of the secret ways *into* the city."

Saida's thoughts raced. She had gone through one of the secret passages before, but she hadn't even thought of it. She hadn't thought that there might be others. The Makali could attack the city and create a distraction while she and Malon went straight for Egrin. Her compass would show her the way to the demon emperor —and to Elmerah.

But then what of their army? Could they both abandon the Makali, leaving them to fight Dreilore and demons? They might be slaughtered. But Elmerah . . .

She brushed her fingers across the circlet at her belt. While her own plans might have changed, her friend's plans had not. Elmerah would go after the emperor herself. And somehow, Saida would ensure that she too was there to see him fall.

Elmerah

E lmerah yawned, forcing one foot after the other. She had never gone to sleep the previous night, instead slowly organizing their departure. It had gone off without a hitch, each one leaving with a few supplies when they would not be noticed. Having Vessa and the elves in on the plan had helped, though Elmerah could have done without Vail's judgmental glares. She was glad to be rid of her.

And not so glad to remain with Rissine.

She glanced over her shoulder down the path to where Rissine and Zirin walked behind her and Alluin.

Further back were Celen and Killian, the former covering up their tracks with his earth-mover magic. The ancient trees of the deepwood surrounded them, casting dappled shadows across the earth.

She felt Alluin watching her as she watched the others. "We did the right thing."

She nodded and turned forward. "I hope Saida understands."

As soon as she had learned about the whistle, she knew she needed to get Rissine away from Saida. She would not give her sister a chance to betray the priestess. Instead, she would use Rissine until the emperor was dead, and then she and her sister could have it out. About *everything*.

She inhaled deeply, scenting a storm on the air. "I just hope I'm right about Malon. He cannot be trusted with many things, but I do believe he will protect her. She is safer with him than with us."

"He has kept her alive thus far," Alluin answered. "Better than we were able to do with Isara."

His words hung heavy in the air. She straightened her fraying coat and kept walking. There was nothing else to do but keep walking forward. She had decided to listen to Malon's advice on the demon portals, not because she thought he cared for her well-being, but because he and Saida knew the demon realm. They would be able to catch up. And there was a good chance none of them could pass through the portals regardless.

She gritted her teeth. Even avoiding the demon

portals, with Saida's compass, they might still catch up. Hopefully with Vessa and the others remaining behind to tell her they'd gone willingly, she would take the hint and not follow.

Alluin put a hand on her arm, startling her out of her thoughts. He held a finger to his lips for her to be quiet, then tapped one pointed ear.

She stopped and listened, catching the occasional sound of voices in the distance. She turned as Zirin and Rissine caught up, gesturing for them to listen too. They all stood still and silent. By the time Celen and Killian reached them, both had already caught on.

Alluin patted Killian's arm, then pointed in the direction of the voices. With a nod, Killian followed him into the trees.

Elmerah's heart pounded as she waited. The only voices one might hear in woods where demons prowled were either Dreilore, or the militia. The Valeroot elves had all escaped south, and no simple farmers or city folk would be risking their necks out here.

Her palms began to sweat, itching to draw her cutlass and go after Alluin. She looked to Rissine, seeing her own worry echoed in her sister's eyes. There was another option for who might be prowling these woods. Surely the Arthali still hunted them both.

Her shoulders relaxed when Alluin and Killian reappeared, heading back toward them. Alluin gestured for them to hurry in the other direction.

Rissine grabbed the sleeve of Elmerah's coat and spun her around, shoving her ahead to go first.

They all moved quietly through the trees for a long while. Elmerah's breathing was harsh by the time she finally stopped and turned to Alluin. "What did you see?"

His green eyes shone with worry. "Some of the same Arthali from Port Aeluvaria, and others, along with a pack of Dreilore. We need to keep moving."

Her fire danced within her at the mention of the traitor Arthali. "We need to go wipe them out."

Rissine shook her head. "They have magic nullifying shackles, and the Dreilore have enchanted blades. We cannot risk it."

"Their blades did them no good against my fire before," she hissed.

Rissine grabbed her arm and squeezed. "And your magic may very well draw demons right to us."

She gnawed her lip. Rissine was right. As much as she wanted to teach the traitorous Arthali a lesson, it wasn't worth it when they had bigger eels to roast. She nodded once.

Rissine looked at each of them. "We must continue on quietly. If the Brambletooth witch picks up our trail, they will hound us all the way to the Capital."

"She picked up your scent the moment you stepped foot on shore," a voice said from ahead.

Rissine moved in front of Elmerah, blocking her view of the woman, but she had seen enough. She remembered Tunisa's curly hair, golden eyes, and magic just like Zirin's.

"I hope you recall what happened the last time you tried to apprehend us," Rissine said evenly.

Elmerah peeked around Rissine's shoulder to see Tunisa crossing her arms and jutting out one hip, her brown leather pants straining against her skin. "Yes, I recall, but I don't see Isara Saredoth amongst you."

Elmerah rested one hand on her cutlass, glancing to Alluin and Celen. If it was just Tunisa, they could easily best her.

Several more Arthali moved in from the surrounding trees. It was warm enough that some had their tattooed arms bare. Elmerah counted three from the Winter Isles clan, like Tunisa and Zirin, two Greenleaf, and one Brambletooth. They would have been no match for two Shadowmarsh witches at full strength, but moving in behind them were Dreilore—and Ayperos. The Dreilore walked beside the giant spiders like they were pets.

Tunisa examined her fingernails, waiting for the sight of the Dreilore and demons to have its full effect. "Dinoba knew you would return to the continent, and he also knew you would make way toward the Capital." She looked up from her fingernails. "Unfortunately for you, Rissine, you are terribly predictable."

Rissine backed up until she was nearly touching Elmerah. "When I tell you to go, I want you to run," she muttered. "I have a plan."

"Not a chance," Elmerah hissed through gritted teeth.

Her fingers wrapped around the hilt of her new cutlass. She could do this. On the island, her fire had not touched her allies. She could cut the Dreilore and enemy Arthali down where they stood.

She started to draw her blade, then her fingers slackened. Her hands reached up to her throat, but she couldn't breathe. She looked frantically to her companions, but she was the only one struggling. Then Rissine fell to her knees in front of her, and she realized it was her sister too.

Someone approached her side as she fought to stay standing, but her vision was beginning to go gray. Finally, she collapsed, then looked up at Egrin Dinoba.

"Your magic is impressive," he said, "but it does not work when you can't draw air."

He was right, she tried to reach for her fire, but it fizzled to ash within her. The Dreilore had closed in around them, and as Elmerah watched, they put magic nullifying shackles on Rissine, binding her hands in front of her.

Egrin let up long enough for Elmerah to draw one harsh breath.

"Reach for your magic, and I'll kill your sister," he said coolly.

Elmerah took another ragged breath into her burning lungs, looking behind her to see the others disarmed and being shackled. She darted her frantic gaze back to Egrin. "Let them go," she rasped. "I'll go with you."

Egrin ignored her. He was looking at Tunisa. "Bring them all to the Capital."

Relief flooded her that at least Egrin would not take her here and now. Then he knelt beside her, wrapping one hand around her arm. Moonstones glittered on his fingers, adding to his magic. He would be more powerful now than when she last faced him.

She cast one final glance at her companions. Alluin's terror for her was a dagger through the heart. On her knees, Rissine was lifting the little silver whistle from around her neck in her shackled hands.

Elmerah thought she heard the whistle's high-pitched call as she and Egrin disappeared in a cloud of darkness.

<hr/>

"**P**ut her in the cage," Egrin ordered the two Dreilore who had descended the stairs of the keep with them.

Elmerah bucked her legs as the Dreilore tugged at her arms. The torches in the windowless stone room flickered wildly with her movements. She tried to reach for her magic, but the shackles cut her off from it.

Her heart screamed at the idea of being put back in a cage, but the Dreilore were strong. They dragged her across the stone floor, then tossed her inside, slamming the grated door shut behind her. The clang of metal echoed through her bones.

With his arms laced behind his back, Egrin

approached the cage. The flickering torchlight cut strange shadows across his face. "You won't be escaping this time, witch. You will help me, or your friends will die."

She staggered to her feet, then pressed her shackled hands against the door to her prison, leaning toward him. "My friends aren't here you white-bellied wyrm."

His mouth twisted into what some might consider a smile. "Their journey will give us time to talk."

She sneered. "I have no desire to converse with a demon."

He leaned even closer, so that his face was nearly touching the bars between them. "You'll do what you're told, or I'll crush the air from your lungs over and over again until you go mad."

"You will be wasting your time," she hissed. "I cannot grant you the secrets to my magic any more than I could explain why the sea exists, or by what trick the stars manage to hang in the sky."

"Yes," he said, stepping back. "I have reached that same conclusion. I cannot pluck your magic from your soul like a moonstone, but your priestess friend gave me a better idea. She was able to draw on the power of the Crown of Cindra to walk the dream realm. Such magic would have been previously out of her reach." He looked her up and down. "I wonder what would happen if I simply drew from your magic, rather than trying to steal it."

"I'm not a moonstone," she spat.

He tilted his head, his eyes roving across her body. "No, you are better than a moonstone. You have a massive well of magic within you. You don't amplify power, you *are* power. If you give it to me willingly, you can join the other Arthali in our alliance. Fight me, and not only will you die, but your friends and sister will die."

She gritted her teeth. There had to be another way. Saida and Malon. They would still be coming toward the Capital with an army of Makali. They could—

A lump formed in her throat. They couldn't do anything. They didn't even know she had been taken because she'd abandoned them. She had only wanted to protect Saida, but now it was clear she needed Saida to protect her. If the only thing Egrin feared was the circlets, then Saida and Malon were her only hope.

"Take some time to consider it," Egrin said. "Help me, save everyone you care about, and join the new Empire . . . or die." He turned and walked stiff-backed toward the door, then left her alone with the two Dreilore.

She knew better than to even try communicating with them. They watched her with predator's eyes. Once Egrin was done with her, they would chew her bones clean.

Alluin

Alluin staggered, his spine itching with the presence of the blade pointed at it. But at least he wasn't in Rissine's shoes, being shoved and kicked by the other Arthali, especially Tunisa.

Rissine's nose was bleeding and she had a fresh bruise blossoming across her jaw. "You're all cowards," she growled. "Egrin Dinoba will kill you all once he has what he wants."

Tunisa gave her a shove from behind, knocking her to her knees. "Oh I don't think he will. We are just as valuable to him as the Dreilore, or even more so, really." She cast a disgusted glance at their Dreilore companions. The Ayperos had scattered into the woods as soon as everyone was shackled.

"Too prideful for your own good," Zirin muttered, earning a kick from one of the other Arthali.

Celen and Killian wisely kept their mouths shut.

Alluin watched it all with a growing feeling of dread. Their situation was dire, but what was happening to Elmerah? He had noticed Rissine blowing into the Akkeri whistle as Elmerah was taken, but then nothing happened.

At least they were being taken to the Capital. At least he had that small hope of seeing Elmerah again. They were walking toward the sea, so there must be a ship waiting for them, that's why they didn't head back toward the camp he and Killian had spied upon.

For now, all he could do was bide his time and look for an opportunity to escape. He hated to think it, but if that would require leaving Rissine and the others behind, he would do it. He would abandon them all if it meant he had some slim chance of prying Elmerah from Egrin's demonic clutches.

CHAPTER ELEVEN

Saida

S aida held her compass out in front of her, leading the way toward their army. She stepped lightly, well aware of her surroundings with Malon walking to her right and Brosod to her left. The other elves followed, speaking amongst themselves words too quiet for her to hear. Which meant they were probably talking about her.

She forced herself not to think about them. The dial on her compass was twitching more frequently now, changing her course. They were getting closer. Something about it felt wrong. She should be leading the way toward Elmerah, not an army—but that wasn't what her friend wanted. She had left intentionally, making it quite clear that she didn't need Saida to save her.

"It's odd," she said to Malon as they walked. "The compass is still leading us roughly east. It should be pointing south. Our army could not have moved so quickly."

"My people move efficiently," Brosod said. "Especially with antlioch. Warriors will take turns running and riding." She gazed outward and took a deep breath. "And with such cool air and plentiful water? The Makali could put any of your armies to shame."

"We will see just how far they have traveled when we reach them," Malon interjected. "And they will likely need rest before marching on the Capital."

Rest. Rest sounded good. Though she doubted she would get as much as she needed. "And after that? After we tear down the Capital and destroy Egrin?"

Malon stopped walking and turned toward her, placing a hand on her arm. "Alluin's plan to make Isara empress was a good one. Now, with both her and Daemon gone, there will be the question of who is to rule. Faerune is far too weakened to be up for the task, and Rissine's Arthali are too few."

She looked up at him pleadingly. There had to be other options. "And what of the Valeroot elves? What of Alluin's people?"

He shook his head. "Better off in Faerune. After all of the distrust Egrin has sewn, the other races of the Capital will never follow elves. *Any* elves."

Brosod cleared her throat, drawing Saida's eye. "In the Helshone, if someone kills the old clan leader, they may take charge of the clan. But if they have no loyal followers, they will soon be killed and replaced. In that way, we choose our own leaders. If someone does not have the support of the people, they will not rule for long. As flawed as Urali was, she had the support of the people."

Malon glanced back at the elves quietly waiting behind them, then turned his gaze to the surrounding shrubs and grass. "Through lies and manipulation, Egrin has the support of the people within the Capital. We will be viewed as villains when our task is done. None of us will rule there, so let them rebuild and elect their own leader if they so choose."

His words made a wave of nausea course through her. She had already seen her homeland torn down, but they would rebuild, they would persevere. Part of her wanted vengeance on the Capital, but it wasn't the people who lived there who had attacked Faerune. It wasn't the fisherman, or the families with small children. "If we aren't going to rebuild, then why tear down the Capital at all? If we have no ruler now to take Egrin's place, then we have no need to threaten the people of Galterra. Perhaps Elmerah's plan to covertly assassinate the emperor is better."

Malon's silver eyes narrowed. "Because Egrin's armies will march from Galterra. On the full moon, they will march to destroy Faerune. We cannot risk Egrin eluding us, only to send his armies forward, so we will attack his armies first. The Capital itself is not the issue. The issue is the Dreilore and the militia. We will face Egrin once that threat is neutralized."

"But the Dreilore—" she began.

"Will fall before the power of the circlets," he finished. "And when Egrin's armies are destroyed, he will have nothing left to threaten us with, and nowhere left to hide."

Her blood went cold at his words. She had known all this. She had known all along what they planned, and in fact she had pushed for it. But now that they were so close, faced with the reality of battle and bloodshed, she wasn't sure she could go through with it. She wanted to kill Egrin, yes, but she didn't want to go to war. If Vessa could show them into the city . . . but that would still leave Egrin the possibility of escape. Once she made it clear she would not bargain with him, his armies would march.

Her one small hope of avoiding such bloodshed was for Elmerah to succeed in assassinating the emperor before the Makali reached the Capital. Though she was worried for her friend, part of her was glad Elmerah had run off ahead. She sent a quiet prayer to Cindra to aid Elmerah in her endeavor, and to guide them all through the trying times ahead.

Elmerah

E lmerah lay curled up in her cage, her back pressed against the bars with her shackled hands tucked under her chin. She wasn't sure how long she had been there, all she knew was that she had given up trying to escape—at least for now. Her Dreilore guards had been changed out several times, she'd lost count of just how many. Sometimes they would march her out to relieve herself, confident the shackles would keep her magic in check.

She wondered how long it would be before Rissine and the others arrived. Egrin must still not be at his full power, even with the moonstones, or else he would have just transported them all here himself.

Or maybe he just wanted to make her wait. To draw out her suffering.

The door leading to her prison opened, making the torches flicker. A female Faerune elf entered, carrying a plate of food. It took Elmerah a moment to realize it was Thera. The last time she had seen the elf was the last time she was in one of Egrin's cages. Elmerah's stomach growled at the scents wafting from the plate. She couldn't remember when she had last eaten.

Thera avoided looking at Elmerah as she approached. Her long, white-blonde hair was pulled back into a tight braid, leaving her gaunt face bare. She looked like she needed the meal upon the tray even more than Elmerah, and she could have it too. As starved as she was, she had no intention of eating the food. It was probably poisoned to weaken her further.

Thera knelt to set the tray of food on the ground just outside the bars where Elmerah might be able to push one hand through far enough to reach it.

Elmerah sat up, observing Thera's frame through her loose black dress. The color didn't suit her. "Serving a demon doesn't seem to agree with you."

Thera's pale eyes darted up. "At least I am alive, and not in a cage."

"Not in an actual cage, but I imagine you're just as trapped as I."

Thera wrinkled her dainty nose. Dark circles marred the skin beneath her eyes. "I'm supposed to look at you and see if any of your magic persists despite your shackles."

Elmerah lifted a brow. "And were you supposed to tell me that?"

Thera shrugged, then stood. "It doesn't matter. Egrin will get what he wants. Neither of us have any choice."

"And what does he want?"

"An empire of demons."

Elmerah shivered. "What did he promise you? Demon magic like he granted the Dreilore?"

Thera sneered. "The magic is limited. They can only access it when Egrin wills it. He could take it away in an instant. Egrin will rule these lands, and none shall stand against him."

The Dreilore guards shifted uneasily. Elmerah would have laughed in their faces if she didn't fear a beating.

She turned her attention back to Thera. "Well I'm glad to see you're trying so hard to stop him," she said caustically.

Thera gave her a dead-eyed stare in response. She shook her head at some silent thought. "What happened to Rissine? The last I heard, the emperor was hunting you both."

Elmerah leaned back against the bars. "So you don't know? Your long-time *friend* will be here soon. The Arthali have her." *And Alluin, and Celen. Gods what a mess.*

"And the priestess?" Thera pressed.

"I don't know where she is," Elmerah lied.

"That's something, at least." Thera stepped back, turning to go.

"Don't tell me you actually care about Saida."

She noticed a slight tightening around Thera's eyes as she turned back to her. "I don't even know the girl. I was just curious. Word around Galterra is that she wields the power of Ilthune and will come to kill us all."

Elmerah snorted. Of course that was the rumor Egrin would choose to spread. "The people of this city are fools."

Thera's eyes darted to the Dreilore guards, then back to Elmerah. "Do you think she's actually a threat?"

Elmerah watched her for a moment. She was quite

sure Thera wasn't asking if Saida was a threat to the city. She was asking if she was a threat to Egrin. If she cared about a threat to Egrin, that meant she wanted him dead.

"Not a threat at all." She gave a slight wink that only Thera could see.

With a quick nod, Thera turned and retreated.

Elmerah watched her go. Perhaps her efforts were in vain, but something had changed with the elf. If there was a single ally to be found in the castle, it was her.

Alluin

Their captors marched them through the rainy night, arriving at the small port damp and exhausted the next morning. The few sailors and workers milling about watched the procession out of the corners of their eyes. No one dared to look directly at any of the Arthali or Dreilore. Alluin noticed a few more bold glances lingering on him, and he wondered when they last saw a Valeroot elf—if any of his people still remained near the Capital.

The Dreilore at his back pressed his blade against Alluin's shirt, prodding him across the wooden dock toward the small ship. Once they were on that ship, they would be taken to the Capital, and escape would be near impossible. The footsteps echoing across the dock seemed to beat in time with his pounding heart.

He looked to Rissine being marched near his side, wondering why her eyes scanned the ocean so intently, almost as if she expected another ship somewhere out there.

"Move," the Dreilore said in a thick accent behind him, and he realized it was his turn to walk the plank up to the small ship.

He moved in front of the plank, then stepped up onto the board, briefly debating throwing himself into the water below. He would have done it if his hands weren't shackled. As it stood, he would do Elmerah no good if he drowned himself.

One by one, they were marched onto the ship, then forced to sit near the main mast. Below, he could barely hear Tunisa exchanging a few words with the portmaster.

He had been seated next to Rissine, who stretched her neck to continue gazing out at the ocean.

"What is it?" he whispered.

She glanced at the Dreilore keeping an eye on them, then shook her head. "Whatever happens, you must reach Elmerah. Even if you have to leave all of us behind."

"I would gladly put her life before any of yours." It was a cruel thing to say, but it was the truth. He knew both Rissine and Celen would do the same thing to him. Maybe not Killian—he would probably get himself killed trying to rescue them all, but he could not afford to make the Nokken a priority.

Once Tunisa was on board, the ship cast off. By his estimations, it would be a short trip to the Capital. If Rissine had some sort of plan, it would have to be enacted soon.

Tunisa moved behind the main mast, using her magic to fill the sails with wind. The water and sea breeze became louder as they picked up speed. The pit of dread in Alluin's stomach swelled.

Killian scooted closer to his other side, opposite Rissine, bumping Alluin's shoulder with his. His russet hair streamed in the breeze across his pinned-back fox ears. "Just in case you have some sort of plan," he muttered, "I figured I should tell you that my hands are not actually shackled. I gave the illusion of them being bound when the emperor took Elmerah, and no one realized they hadn't actually captured me."

His words were too low for anyone else to hear, but that didn't keep Alluin from glancing around warily.

No one paid them any mind. So they had one ally unbound, for what good it would do them. It would have been more useful to have someone with real magic, not just illusion limited to himself.

"If you can escape," he muttered back, "do it. Find Saida and let her know what has happened."

Killian blinked amber eyes at him, then nodded.

Alluin found himself surprised that he believed Killian would do as promised. He never would have thought in one million years he would grow to trust a Nokken, but here they were.

"Ship ahead!" one of their captors called out.

Alluin glanced back to see Tunisa rolling her eyes. "It's surely just militia this close to the Capital!" she shouted back.

"Akkeri!" another Arthali shouted.

"Be ready," Rissine said, bumping Alluin's shoulder.

He glanced down at the silver whistle hanging from her neck. His jaw fell open. "You summoned them, didn't you? Merwyn recognized that whistle."

Rissine gave him a wry grin. "It seemed the circumstances called for it."

The Arthali and Dreilore hurried around them, preparing for the Akkeri ship heading their way.

"What did you promise Hotrath in exchange?" Alluin demanded. "Did you say you would give him Saida?"

She smirked. "My, you do catch on quick. Oh, don't look at me like that. I'm not really going to give him the priestess. We will figure it out once we are—"

The impact from a cannonball rocked the ship. Tunisa cursed, sending her winds toward the Akkeri. If the ship sunk with their hands still bound, they would drown.

Alluin whipped his attention toward Killian. "Tunisa has the key for our shackles."

Killian nodded. In the blink of an eye, a male Dreilore had taken Killian's place. He hopped to his feet and ran off without another word.

More cannon fire sounded.

"Were his hands free this whole time?" Rissine asked, sounding much too calm given the circumstances.

"Never underestimate a Nokken," Celen said from somewhere behind them.

Alluin ignored them both. With the ship wildly rocking, he had lost track of which Dreilore was actually Killian. Then one of the Dreilore bumped into Tunisa's back. She cursed at him, but was too busy maintaining her winds to realize the keys had gone missing from her belt.

Killian returned to them a moment later, still in his Dreilore disguise.

"Rissine first," Alluin ordered.

Killian nodded and unlocked her shackles.

Rissine rubbed her wrists and stood. "The rest of you abandon ship. I will cover your escape."

One of the enemy Arthali ran past them, then skidded to a halt. "Hey!" he grabbed for Rissine.

His hands now free, Zirin punched the man in the face, knocking him out cold.

Killian freed Alluin last. They all stood close together, waiting for someone else to notice them.

"Over the railing at the back of the ship," Rissine ordered. "Now!"

Alluin considered for a moment that Elmerah would not want him to leave her sister behind, but at least one of them had to escape. He turned and ran toward the back of the ship.

He was almost at the railing when a Dreilore jumped in his path. He dove aside, avoiding the Dreilore's blade, then rolled across the deck and came to his feet.

A gust of strong wind sent the Dreilore careening sideways.

Alluin nodded his thanks to Zirin, scaled the railing, then dove into the sea.

Icy water slammed into him, stealing his breath. He dove deeper, propelling himself away from the ship. It would only take one Dreilore arrow to thwart his escape, so he stayed under. Until they reached shore, they were all on their own.

He kicked underwater until his lungs screamed for air, then finally he surfaced, daring a quick glance back at the ship. With Arthali winds deflecting most of the cannonballs, the ship was still afloat, but the Akkeri now drew near, preparing to board. That was the last he saw of it as he turned away and continued swimming toward shore.

A moment later, fox ears popped up in the water beside him, followed by Killian's dripping wet face. "I don't think Zirin and Rissine made it off the ship. They fought the Dreilore so Celen and I could get away."

"Just keep swimming," he panted. "There's nothing we can do for them now."

Despite his words, he briefly debated going back. If Elmerah survived long enough to learn that he left her sister for dead, it would surely be the end for them all.

CHAPTER TWELVE

Alluin

"Keep moving," Alluin ordered, seeing that Celen and Killian were beginning to slow. He understood that they were tired—he was worn to the bone himself—but they had already lost too much time. He knew what Egrin had done to Elmerah when he captured her before. He couldn't just leave her to that fate again.

"We need a plan," Celen argued. "We'll reach Galterra in the morning. How do we intend to reach Ellie? My magic can only get us so far, and we have nothing to prevent that demon from crushing the air out of us."

He stopped walking, looking back at Celen and

Killian. Their clothes had dried, but both looked haggard and about ready to fall over. "I know how to get into the city unnoticed."

Celen walked toward him, swiping a palm across his scarred face and back into his short hair. He smelled like the ocean and sweat. "And into the keep? The dungeon? Wherever she is being held?"

Alluin didn't have an answer for him. He'd never been within the main castle. "We can't just leave her there."

"Saida—"

He shook his head, cutting Celen off. "She would have gone after her army by now. We don't know how to find her."

Killian moved closer, his fox ears pinned back against his hair. His amber eyes were hooded, wary. "I'll go. I can disguise myself and find a way into the castle. If I can locate my sister—"

Celen gave Killian a warning glance. "You don't know that she's still there, or that she'll even help you. She *volunteered* to work with the emperor after he threatened your people."

Killian's pointy chin lowered. "I know, but if I can simply explain things to her—"

"No," Alluin said. "Even if we can find her, we don't know that we can trust her. We can't risk her turning us in before we reach Elmerah."

Killian straightened. "Well I'll still go. I can get into

the castle. I'll find a path to Elmerah. She's my friend too."

He considered the Nokken's offer. He highly doubted Elmerah thought him a friend in return, let alone someone who should be trusted with her life. Sending Killian ahead would mean putting every ounce of trust he had into someone he had only recently gotten to know . . . but what other choice did he have? Killian had saved their necks on the ship, and he had saved them before in Aeluvaria.

He glanced around at the slowly darkening trees. If they kept walking, they could reach Galterra that very night. "Alright," he decided, "I'll get us into the city, and you'll get us into the keep. With any luck Saida's army will arrive and provide a distraction."

"We have no weapons," Celen argued. "We don't even have cloaks to hide our appearance."

Alluin's gut clenched at the thought of pillaging any belongings left behind by his people, but he knew some of the camps had been hastily abandoned. Some useful items might remain. "I know where we may be able to find some supplies." *Supplies left behind because too many had been lost, and not everything could be carried.*

Celen watched him for a moment, clearly wondering, but he didn't question Alluin's offer. "Lead on then." He hesitated. "I don't like the idea of what's happening to Ellie either, you know."

"I know." He nodded. "We'll get her back." *Again. She was lost again. As hard as he tried, he just kept losing her.*

It was a habit he fully intended to break.

Rissine

The image of Tunisa tied to the main mast with shackles on her wrists was something Rissine hoped to remember for the rest of her life. The few other surviving Arthali and Dreilore were shackled too, all seated on the deck while Hotrath decided if it was worth keeping them alive.

Glancing at the High King, she stepped a little closer to Zirin. The Akkeri had kept their part of the bargain, now they would expect her to deliver Saida. What might they do when she told them she had no idea where the elven priestess was? Whatever they chose, there would be no escaping them. Several more ships loomed in the distance, slowly closing in. Hotrath had promised an army, and he had delivered.

She startled when she realized the High King was watching her.

"You don't seem to have my payment." He raised a massive bare brow at her.

The other Akkeri who had boarded the ship chattered around him, some poking spears at their new captives. The rage in one female Dreilore's eyes gave Rissine the chills. The Akkeri had shackled a pack of wolves, and Rissine hoped they knew better than to ever free them.

She gnawed her lip, realizing Hotrath was still waiting for a reply. *Think, Rissine, think.* "She will be delivered once I have finished using your army."

Hotrath gave her an irritated smile. "Is that so? What else would you have of us?"

The surrounding Akkeri had her so unnerved, she blurted the first thing that came to mind. "We must attack Galterra and rescue my sister from Egrin Dinoba."

"You fool," Tunisa interrupted. "As if the Akkeri could take the Capital. If they had such numbers they would have pillaged the city long ago."

Hotrath burst out laughing, the sound surprisingly rich and throaty. "You are brazen, witch, but I will need proof that you can provide the priestess, separated from the circlet, of course."

Rissine glanced at Zirin, then the captive Arthali. She did not like divulging any information in front of the latter, but she had a feeling she was running out of time to bargain. "Saida marches toward the Capital with an army of Makali warriors. She intends to use the circlets to destroy Egrin Dinoba. Once that has been accomplished, it would be the perfect time to catch her unaware. She trusts me enough. I could get close to her."

Hotrath moved closer, his footsteps heavy on the deck. He loomed a full head taller than her, casting her in shadow. "You want us to attack the Capital, a well fortified city protected by Dreilore, demons, and the militia?"

Her mouth went dry. "Surely demons do not protect the city."

"If Dinoba summons them, they will come."

She crossed her arms, gripping her flesh tightly through her torn emerald coat. If the Akkeri and Makali attacked at the same time, and were met with Dreilore, the militia, and demons . . . it would be a bloodbath.

But it might also be just the distraction she needed to reach Elmerah.

She pretended to think things over for a moment, then nodded. "Yes, that is what I would like you to do. Help me rescue my sister, and I will do everything in my power to deliver Saida and the circlet to you." She felt ill just making the offer. Elmerah was never going to forgive her, but at least she would be alive.

Hotrath studied her face. "And what of our captives?" He extended one meaty palm toward the bound Arthali.

Rissine shrugged. "Throw them overboard for all I care."

Hotrath stepped so close his fishy odor was overwhelming. "No, I think I will hang onto them for now. If you betray me, I will give you to them." He glanced at Tunisa, then back to her. "I think that one has something truly terrible planned for you."

Rissine sucked her teeth. After the humiliation Tunisa had suffered, she really would cut Rissine into tiny bits, but it was still better than what the Dreilore might do to her.

She held out a hand toward Hotrath. She would have to worry about that later, just as she would worry about Saida later. For now, more Akkeri ships appeared in the distance. The Capital was not far. Egrin would rue the day he decided to cross Shadowmarsh witches.

Hotrath seemed surprised for a moment by her offer, then he took her hand and shook it. His skin was damp and clammy. "I cannot wait to see the look on Dinoba's face."

She could hardly even imagine it. "You and me both," she breathed, hoping she wasn't making the biggest mistake of her life.

Saida

S aida stood near Vessa and the other elves as they took in their army. The Makali had made tremendous progress, reaching an area of the woods over halfway between Galterra and Aeluvaria. There would be no going back now. Tomorrow they would march on the Capital.

Brosod had gone with Malon to meet with the clan leaders.

Vessa huddled close to Saida in the tree shadows. "Are you sure we can trust them?" she whispered.

"They will do as we ask," she whispered back.

Her army would march on the Capital and cut down any in their path. Then they would take the city, and she would hunt down Egrin Dinoba. She still could hardly face the thought of war, but she had been convinced it was a necessary evil. She would not let the armies march upon Faerune. Without his city or his armies, Egrin could not hide from her forever.

"I don't like that scary look in your eye," Vessa muttered.

Saida blinked, pulling out of her thoughts. "Once we reach the city, you can do what you want. You don't have to follow me."

Vessa shook her hair out of her face. "What I want is to find my brother. And that's what you should want too. That's why he left me behind. Let me show you into the city." She glanced at Vail, standing quietly at her other side.

Vail met her gaze as some silent question passed between them. After a moment, the healer inclined her chin. "I agree. Your quarrel is with the emperor, and Alluin may need your help. You should come with us."

The three male elves accompanying them did not comment, though she had noticed their gazes lingering

184

on the other elves who marched with the Makali—Malon's early recruits. Perhaps the Valeroot elves were wishing they had made better alliances from the start.

She almost wanted to take Vail and Vessa up on their offer. Malon's plan was logical, but it didn't cover Alluin and Elmerah reaching the Capital before them. If they went after the emperor, they might need her help.

She didn't have a chance to answer before Malon and Brosod returned to them.

"We will rest for half the night," Malon explained as he reached her, "then we will begin our march in darkness. If my estimations are correct, we will reach Galterra at first light. I hope you have not reconsidered our plan." He gave her a knowing look.

She glanced at the elves. "We cannot allow his armies to leave the Capital. Once we have taken the city, we will go after the emperor."

Vessa shook her head, clearly disappointed. "If you do not come with us, Egrin will be warned of your arrival. What if he simply disappears in a cloud of darkness and evades you?"

She patted her belt pouch where her compass rested. "I will follow him to the ends of the earth if need be."

Malon stepped closer and placed a hand upon her shoulder. "Hopefully it will not come to that. I only wish Elmerah had not lost Isara."

Saida bowed her head. "What's done is done. We must do what we can to protect Faerune."

He squeezed her shoulder, then stepped away. "We should rest while we can. Tomorrow, we end this."

She glanced at the other elves, all watching on. Tomorrow would be the end of all they had worked for, one way or another.

Isara

"I don't know why you insist on exploring this blasted island," Daemon said behind Isara as they both trudged through the sand.

She knew better than to explain it to him. They had come across the demon carcasses the day before. They must have come from *somewhere*, and she intended to find out. No ships large enough to carry them to the mainland had docked since their arrival, and she was not content to live out her days on the tiny island with her brother.

Although, she had considered it. On this island, they could live in peace. Her brother's duties to Egrin did not exist here, nor did her promises.

She almost slowed her steps across the sand, then she shook her head and picked up her pace. She was not a coward, not anymore. Those demons had found some way onto the island, which meant there was another way off of it.

She would find it. She would escape, and would take Daemon with her, even if she had to drag him by his ear the entire way.

CHAPTER THIRTEEN

Alluin

They found rest at an abandoned Valeroot settlement. Alluin could still picture all of the elves there, forging rough weapons, restringing bows, sharing a morning meal. Now they were all gone. Those who hadn't fled were killed. He didn't know how many, and he hoped to never find out.

He stood alone in one of the wooden huts. He had already searched it for supplies, but most had been pilfered. While he had found a dusty cloak to wear, he found no weapons or food. The food they could do without—both he and Killian we're skilled hunters and knew how to live off the land—but the weapons were a problem. Could they really hope to free Elmerah with Celen's magic alone?

He didn't think so, but it wouldn't stop him from trying.

"Are you ready?" Celen stood in the open doorway, framed in the smoky purple light of early dawn.

He nodded, then followed Celen out of the hut. He wished they could have entered the Capital under the cover of night, but they had desperately needed rest. At least Celen and Killian hadn't asked any questions about the settlement. They both seemed to understand that he wouldn't want to talk about it.

Killian waited at the edge of the settlement, his back to them as he kept watch. His simple tunic and breeches were dirty and torn, but he could easily cast an illusion to make them look brand new.

As he approached Killian's back, he wondered what the Nokken actually thought about things. He'd followed Celen on impulse, and had been practically forced into their plan. Killian looked up to Celen like some sort of idol, and he ended up the only one of his people actually striving against the emperor. Alluin could relate. Yes, Vessa had followed him, but she never would have fought for the Valeroot elves on her own. He no longer begrudged her choices. Perhaps she was wiser than him after all.

Celen walked at Alluin's side. "You're sure you can get us into the city unnoticed?"

He nodded, though his blood felt like ice in his veins.

The closest entrance was the same way he and Elmerah once fled, leaving the burning corpses of his kin behind. He wasn't even sure if the underground path was accessible now, but it was their best choice. Either that, or lose another day traveling to a different secret entrance.

Celen gestured for Killian to follow as they walked past.

"It's not far from here," Alluin explained, "but keep your senses about you. One of the Dreilore found us there before. She did not survive, but I cannot guarantee others don't know about the place. If they didn't keep it for their own, they might have caved it in."

"I can take care of a simple cave-in." Celen pulled up the hood of his pilfered brown cloak. It was in far worse condition than the one Alluin had found, but at least it would conceal his features.

Alluin looked in the direction they would be heading. It would take an hour, maybe less. He had no idea what they would do if they managed to not only enter the city, but the keep. They would simply have to figure it out when it happened.

Elmerah

Elmerah barely had time to react as the door to her cage swung open, then Egrin fisted his hand in her hair. She had finally managed a few moments of sleep, and this was what it got her.

He dragged her across the stone floor. She glanced around frantically, realizing they were alone. There were no Dreilore guards to watch them.

Her scalp felt on fire as Egrin lifted her by her hair until she was on her feet, then leaned in next to her cheek. "Tell me what they're planning."

She stood on her boot tips, swaying dangerously, lest he yank her hair out by the root. "What are you talking about!"

Using her hair, he tossed her across the room. With her hands still shackled she landed hard on her shoulder. Pain shot through her, but she forced herself to roll over.

Not fast enough. His boot landed against her abdomen, stealing her breath.

She curled up, choking and gagging.

He stood over her with his boots right next to her face. "What. Are. They. *Planning?*"

She glared up at him. "Who? The gods? The fates? I couldn't tell you."

He crouched down beside her. "There is an entire fleet of Akkeri ships sailing in from the west. Any moment now they will launch their attack upon my port. It would not be such an issue if those blasted elves weren't standing outside my gates with an army of

Makali." He grabbed her hair again, pulling her face toward his. "How did they enlist the Akkeri?"

She blinked at him. *The Makali.* That meant Saida was here.

He dragged her up again, then started walking toward the door. "I had planned to wait for the full moon. Everything would have worked out perfectly, but now we have to rush."

She stumbled after him, her scalp screaming in pain. "Rush what!"

Thera stood just outside the doorway with a tray of food. She staggered back, spilling the tray. Her wide eyes locked with Elmerah's.

"Come," Egrin ordered her. "You'll be needed."

He continued through the keep, and Elmerah realized past her pain that it was eerily quiet. Not one human nor Dreilore lurked. They were entirely alone.

"Where are you taking me?" she demanded.

"I won't risk those elves finding us before we're done. I'll just have to fetch Isara later."

She stumbled after him, bent at an odd angle with his lowered hand tugging her hair. "Isara?"

"She'll be needed, but not yet."

They rounded a bend with Thera scurrying after them. "Saida and Malon will find you," she threatened. "You fear them."

He spun around, slamming her against the wall before pressing a hand around her throat. He leaned in near her face. "The circlets will not be a threat for long. I would advise you to keep your mouth shut and do as you're told."

He released her only long enough to shove her ahead of him, but she hadn't missed the fear in his eyes. He really was afraid of Saida, but she was still outside the gates. There was still time for him to achieve whatever he had set out to do.

He continued to shove her until they reached a room at the end of a long hall. Egrin stopped before a hatch in the ground. Lightning fast, he grabbed her hair again, dragging her down with him as he opened the hatch with his free hand.

Elmerah stared through the opening. Nothing but darkness stared back.

Egrin let go of her hair. "Down."

She stepped back. "I don't think so."

He grabbed her arm, dragging her toward the hatch. "Climb down the ladder, or I will throw you down, and break every bone in your body. I don't care if you're crippled, I only need you alive."

He looked to Thera. "Find Lord Orius. Bring him here. Tell him it is time to make good on his end of the bargain."

He shoved Elmerah toward the hatch again. "Now climb, or fall. I don't care. Either way you're going *down.*"

She gave Thera a pleading look, but the elf only stepped back, still clutching her empty tray.

"Down!" Egrin shouted.

"I can't climb a ladder in shackles!" she shouted back, holding out her hands.

He merely touched her shackles and they fell away, clattering to the stone floor. "Summon your magic, and you know what will happen."

She did know. She wouldn't summon it, not until it was her last resort. She stepped toward the hatch and started climbing. If she was going to find a way out of this, she preferred to do it without broken bones.

Thera turned away and fled, leaving Egrin alone to watch her descent.

She continued down into the darkness, fighting the warning voice in her head that told her she would never come back up.

Isara

Isara stared down into the gaping pit, wrinkling her nose at a strange smell emanating from within. Her body was coated with sweat, her limbs trembling. She had spent the morning clearing rocks and dirt out of the hole. It was no natural cavern, she could sense it. The incline was steep, but it would be possible to climb down into that darkness.

"This has to be where the demons came from."

Daemon moved to her side, his eyes wide as he looked down. "And remind me again why we care where the demons came from?"

"Maybe we can use the passage to get off this island."

He stepped back. "You foolish girl. I humored your search because we have nothing better to do, but you're speaking absolute madness. We are safe here, we have food and shelter."

She wiped the sweat from her brow, then crossed her shaking arms, waiting for him to calm down. "I think it's time you told me what you're hiding."

He raked a hand through his curls, his fingers snagging in the tangles. He tugged his hand back out in a jerky, irritated movement. "I don't know what you're talking about."

She waited patiently, noticing a cool gust of air easing its way up from the cavern. Birds sang happily around them. Whatever evil had come up from the cavern was long gone, but that did not mean it was safe. If the cavern led to the demon realm, something else could come upon it from below at any moment.

"You would never simply be content to live out your life on this island, gutting fish to earn your next meal. I know you're trying to keep me here for a reason."

He glared at her. "Some things you're better off not knowing. Just know that I am trying to keep you safe."

"From what?"

He rolled his eyes. "A horrible death."

She took a step toward him, away from the cavern.

"Egrin ordered you to keep me here, didn't he? Why did he do it? What does he want with me?"

Daemon tried to stare her down, but she wouldn't look away. Not this time.

"Fine," he huffed. "We are here for safekeeping. When Egrin needs us, he will come."

Her mind flooded with emotions, overwhelming her better senses. She marched right up to him and slapped him across the face.

His eyes flared as he gripped his cheek. "You've got to stop doing that, you foolish girl. The only reason you're alive is because I bargained with him to keep you alive."

"Are you so blind? Or can you simply not see me as anything of value? I'm still alive because Egrin wants to use me in some way. I'm the only person who can nullify his magic. If he didn't need me, he would have killed me at the start. If we wait here for him, eventually he will take me, use me, then get rid of me."

Still clutching his cheek, he stared at her unblinking.

She sighed heavily. "You've never been one to think things through." But then she realized he wasn't staring *at* her, but past her.

She turned around, then gasped. A dozen creatures with shaggy gray hair and onyx eyes watched them. The Fogfaun were small, smaller than her, with goat-like legs and humanoid torsos. Their skin was a similar color to their dark gray fur.

"What in the gods are they?" Daemon whispered behind her.

She held up a hand to silence him, then took a step toward the creatures. She remembered their magic, how they could easily abduct people . . . "We need your help. Can you transport us off this island?"

The closest creature tilted its head, then pointed to the cavern. "Did you make hole?"

Oh gods, not this again. They must have come to investigate the cavern. "Listen," she began, daring to move a step closer. "The weather worker is trying to get rid of the demon king, but she needs my help. Can you take me to her?"

"Get away from those creatures," Daemon hissed as the Fogfaun began chattering amongst themselves. He grabbed her arm and tried to pull her backward, but she tugged away from him.

The chatter died down as the nearest creature observed her. "Weather worker is with demon king."

She clutched a hand to her chest. Egrin had Elmerah? She cast a glare back at Daemon. "Did you know that Egrin had her?"

"Who? The witch? I had no idea, though it's about time."

Saving her anger for her brother for later, she turned back to the Fogfaun. "Can you help me reach her? I swear to you, we are trying to set things right. We don't want more demons coming up through these holes either."

The creatures all stared at her.

She held her hands together in front of her chest.

"Please. Egrin will kill her, then all of our hopes will be dashed. Together, she and I can defeat him."

The lead creature finally blinked, then inclined its pointy chin.

"Isara," Daemon warned, his voice low.

The other Fogfaun shuffled closer, as if by some silent command. The lead creature began to chant. Isara could feel magic building.

Daemon grabbed her again. "Isara, don't—"

Then everything went black and foggy. When Isara opened her eyes, she was standing upon the shore. But not the shore of the small island. She looked northward, and there stood the tall walls of the Capital.

Daemon cursed emphatically at her side, drawing her attention to him.

She looked her pathetic brother up and down. "I do believe that in your own ridiculous way you were trying to keep me safe, but that ends now. Either you help me defeat him, or you are my brother no more."

He spat in the sand. "We stand no chance of defeating him. I know what you're capable of, and it is not this."

She clenched her hands into fists at her sides. "No, Daemon, you don't know me at all. You never did."

But he was looking right past her again.

Her temper flaring, she followed his gaze out toward the sea as an entire fleet of ships came into view on the horizon. *Akkeri ships.* Distantly, in the other direction, she thought she could hear sounds of fighting already happening. It seemed she had come not a moment too soon.

She turned away from her brother and started running toward the Capital. There were many secret ways into the city, and she knew them all. Her father had never trusted Egrin, and had taught her well. She was done hiding. It was time to show everyone *exactly* what she was capable of.

CHAPTER FOURTEEN

Alluin

The metal grate leading to the tunnel was nothing but twisted ruin. Alluin could not tell if it was a natural cave-in caused by Elmerah's fire weakening the supports, or if Egrin had sealed up the secret path into the city. Most likely the latter. The Dreilore had found the place before, slaughtering his uncle and other kin. Egrin knew about it, and he was not the type of man to leave any weakness in his defenses.

Celen looked over the rubble skeptically. "I can move a lot of it, but if the tunnel is caved in all the way through, there may be too much to clear out."

Part of him wanted to just turn and walk away. Even if the tunnel was still stable within, he did not want to once more walk through the secret hideout. He didn't want to face what had happened. But he had a feeling Elmerah was running out of time. He couldn't leave her trapped with Egrin.

"Clear out the entrance, and we'll reevaluate from there." He moved away from the rubble to stand near Killian out of the way.

Killian watched on, his amber eyes shining with excitement. "Celen's magic is truly amazing."

Alluin didn't have the heart to reply.

Celen lifted his hands. The earth trembled, then began to move, small chunks of rock and rubble at first, then larger mounds of dirt. His magic really was quite the sight. Not as showy as Elmerah's, but impressive just the same. He understood why the Arthali were hated—hunted. Just a few powerful witches were as good as an army.

The earth shook more violently as Celen lifted larger pieces of rubble. Dust clouded the air, making Alluin gag. He could only hope Egrin could not sense the building magic.

More earth poured outward, then the tunnel entrance was clear. The supports were still stable within. He stepped forward, then stopped as the hairs rose on the back of his neck. The scrape of hairy legs echoed out of the dark tunnel.

He cursed, but it was too late, the shadowy form of the first hulking spider neared the tunnel's edge. Egrin had filled the space with Ayperos, or maybe they had gravitated there on their own. It didn't really matter how they got there.

The spider hissed, lunging toward Celen.

He reacted quickly, raising one arm then closing his hand into a fist. The earth shot up around the spider, swallowing it whole, but there was another one to take its place.

"Alluin!" someone shouted behind him. He thought he recognized his sister's voice, but he could not turn as the next spider leapt toward him. He rolled away, and the spider let out a hiss of air as it hit the earth.

He got to his feet, prepared to meet his end, but there was an arrow sticking out of one of the spider's many eyes.

"Alluin!" his sister shouted again, reaching him. The other elves he'd left behind came soon after, ignoring him as they fired bows at the spiders, saving Killian just before he would have been crushed. Merwyn hobbled after them, breathing heavily and looking like he might topple over.

More arrows sailed, Celen made the earth rumble, and then it was over. Dying spiders twitched their limbs in the slowly clearing dust. All was silent from within the tunnel.

Alluin turned and pulled his sister into a fierce hug.

Holding her bow out in one hand, she didn't seem to know what to do with the sudden display of affection. She patted his back with her free hand. "I'm glad we caught you. We couldn't convince Saida to come with us."

"I didn't expect you to," he breathed. "I just wanted you out of harm's way, but it seems I have lured you right into the thick of it."

Vessa laughed, then pulled away. "You know me, I'm impossible to keep out of trouble. And I'm not suited to marching with an army of Makali."

"Saida found them? How far are they?"

"They will reach the city soon. We traveled with them most of the way here, they spared us some supplies." She hefted her bow.

Alluin let out a weak laugh, glancing toward Celen and Killian. Both seemed unharmed, though Killian had spider silk trailing from his ears. Merwyn moved to stand near Killian, who seemed thrilled to see him. If Merwyn's odor bothered the Nokken's sensitive nose, he did not show it.

Vessa patted Alluin's shoulder. "Come now, aren't we here to save your lady love?"

His cheeks grew hot. Had he been so obvious? He caught Vail watching him and quickly looked away.

Celen snorted. "Well I'm glad someone finally had the guts to say it."

Alluin pinched his brow and shook his head. There was no time to argue, and he wasn't sure he wanted to. He greeted the other elves who had just rescued him once again, while he still didn't know their names. But there was no time for introductions now. Elmerah was waiting.

He turned to his sister. "I cannot tell you what we might find within the tunnel. What might be left."

Her expression darkened. She understood. She reached out and took his hand. "We'll get through it."

"When did you become so mature?"

She smirked. "When my brother took it upon himself to overthrow the Empire."

He turned toward the entrance of the tunnel. It was pitch black, but he knew the way well. "Whatever happens, we will make sure our kin did not die in vain."

The other elves, including Vail, muttered their agreement.

"Moving on," Celen said impatiently. "Elmerah needs us. I won't have Rissine coming after me once she escapes those Akkeri."

Vessa looked a question at Alluin.

"I'll explain what happened as we go. Time is short."

Vessa nodded, and they walked into the tunnel together. He'd known he would have to face this eventually. He had hoped Elmerah would be with him, but for now, she was the one who needed *him*.

The others followed them bravely into the tunnel, and soon Merwyn moved to the head of the line. With even just a hint of light he could see well in the darkness, and could warn of any obstructions or craters.

Alluin listened to the Akkeri's steps just ahead of him as he explained to Vessa what had happened with

Rissine. Between his words, memories flashed through his mind. His parents had been gone so long he hardly remembered them, but his uncle, and the others he'd been close to . . . he crept through the dark, remembering their faces. The others followed, occasionally offering observations about the Makali army.

They reached the end of the tunnel with no further incidents. He ran his palms across the surface of the door, accidentally bumping into Merwyn. He tested the handle, finding it unlocked. With the cave-in, no one had bothered to seal the way through. He opened the door without allowing himself time to think, and was glad to find it just as dark as the tunnel had been.

He took the lead, feeling his way along the wall, cutting a wide path around the room. It might have been easier to walk straight through, but he wanted to avoid the center where the bodies had been piled for burning. He didn't explain to the others what they were passing, but judging by their silence, they knew. Vail and Vessa had grown close—she had probably filled the other elves in. And Elmerah might have mentioned it to Celen.

He was overwhelmed with relief to reach the other side of the room where he headed up the stairs. They had been charred and weakened by Elmerah's fire, and groaned beneath his weight. "Watch your step," he cautioned the others behind him.

He reached the top of the stairs and opened another door. The broken windows of the next room let in weak rays of sunlight. The Dreilore they had killed was gone—

everything was gone—left to ruin and dust. Dark stains still marred the floor where the elves had fallen.

A sound behind him drew his eye.

Vessa held a hand over her mouth, choking back tears. She shook her head, her attention lingering on the stains. "I knew what happened, it's just—"

"Seeing it is different," he finished for her.

Celen and the others waited behind her quietly, understanding that now was not the time to interrupt.

Alluin didn't want to rush her, but— "Time is short. There is nothing to be done here."

Her hand still covering her mouth, she nodded too quickly.

Vail caught Alluin's eye as she stepped forward, wrapping one arm around Vessa's shoulder.

He nodded his thanks, then walked across the room and stepped outside. While the back street was usually secluded, now it was utterly deserted. He could hear the sound of distant fighting.

As the others crowded around him, he gazed in the direction of the castle. "Celen and Killian with me." He glanced at the elves. "The rest of you, find out what's going on in the city. Once we have Elmerah, we will need to plan a route of escape to Saida."

"But we just found you!" Vessa blurted.

Vail placed a hand on her shoulder. "He's right. Once they have Elmerah, the emperor will come after them. They can lead him to face Malon's army. We will make sure the path is clear."

Merwyn pulled back his hood, revealing his sickly face and nearly bald head. While he was normally looking at his own feet, now he met Alluin's gaze unwaveringly. "I will go with you."

Alluin felt pity for the small creature, but Merwyn was weak and slow. "You will only hinder us. You should find Saida."

"I will look after myself. Saida will find *you*. Saida will find Elmerah."

"But she is with her army," Vessa countered.

Merwyn didn't argue with her. His attention remained on Alluin. "I have faith she will come."

"We don't have time for this," Celen interrupted. "Let him come."

He was right. "Fine," Alluin agreed. "Let's go."

Vessa gnawed her lip, but didn't argue further. She knew the hidden ways through the city, she could lead the elves. And he knew the way to the castle. Unable to bring himself to say goodbye, perhaps for the last time, he simply nodded to Celen and Killian, then led the way down the deserted street.

Saida

S aida coughed on the thick smoke, scented of burning flesh. Power surged through her. It had been so easy. With Malon beside her, unleashing the magic of the circlets was as simple as breathing.

"This isn't right," she muttered more to herself than to anyone else. Whispers coming from the circlet drowned out her voice, but she knew she was the only one who could hear them. She could not make out the words, but her instincts told her it was a warning. It was not the gods' will for her to go into battle in this way. Not Cindra's will, at least.

The first wave of the assault had ended, and their enemies lay dead and dying at their feet. Even the Ayperos and other demons that had fought alongside the Dreilore. Ancient monsters, defeated like they were nothing. She understood now why Egrin had avoided direct confrontation.

Malon gripped her hand, his eyes pinched as he peered through the clearing smoke. The Crown of Arcale upon his brow glowed with luminescent light.

The Dreilore and militia hadn't stood a chance. She wondered if Vessa and the elves had made it into the city.

"It's time to advance." Malon stepped toward the Makali ranks, pulling her along.

She resisted, tugging her hand out of his.

He turned toward her, his confusion clear. Flakes of ash mingled with his silver hair. The next soldiers would be more wary after what she and Malon had done. "What's wrong?"

She lifted trembling fingers toward the circlet upon her head, then stopped herself. "Don't you hear the whispers? This isn't what we're supposed to be doing."

He stepped close to her. Their warriors were waiting for further orders. The rest of their opponents were now shut up in the city walls. She and Malon would be needed to tear those walls down.

"It's just nerves. We are doing what we must to protect Faerune."

"But you don't care about protecting Faerune."

He gently gripped both her arms. "But you do. This was not my plan, Saida. This was your plan."

It was, wasn't it? Or had he manipulated her?

"We can't let them regather inside. We must attack now."

Brosod approached from within the Makali ranks. A small cut on her cheek dripped blood, but she was otherwise unharmed. Even with the circlets, the Makali were needed to keep them from being overwhelmed by Egrin's sheer numbers. "We await orders," she said, looking to Saida.

She squeezed her eyes shut, unable to make a decision. Her skin felt cold. The whispers were nearly deafening. She tried to listen to them, tried to pick any one voice out. She placed her fingers on the circlet, then a single voice became clear, rising above the rest. *She needs your help. Go to her. I will guide you.*

Her eyes flew wide. She dove forward, clutching Malon's arms. "I must reach Elmerah. Something is wrong."

"You don't know where she is."

She stepped away from him. "You do what you must, I understand. But this is not the task I was meant for."

Brosod realized her intent before Malon did. She lunged for Saida, grabbing on just as she was engulfed in a flash of moonlight.

One moment she was looking at Malon's shocked expression, and the next she was standing in a quiet courtyard with Brosod. Manicured shrubs loomed around them, but nothing moved.

"Where are we?" Brosod gasped.

Saida's body trembled. She recognized the courtyard. She had been here before, the day Thera kidnapped her and gave her to Egrin. But this time there were no militia men to drag her inside. There was no one at all. She could hear distant fighting in the city, but the castle grounds were utterly silent.

"Saida," someone whispered from a nearby shrub.

She and Brosod turned. Brosod hefted her spear as a young man in servant's garb revealed himself.

Saida stepped back beside Brosod. "Do I know you?"

The young man appeared momentarily confused. "Oh. Hold on." His dark hair turned red, and fox ears flicked forward.

"Killian!" she gasped. She never thought she would be so relieved to see someone she barely knew. Gesturing for Brosod to lower her spear, she hurried toward him. "Where is Elmerah?" She really had heard the voices in the circlet. They had not led her astray. If Killian was here, Elmerah must be nearby.

Before he could answer, more footsteps sounded, drawing her attention toward three cloaked figures.

Brosod lifted her spear again, then lowered it slightly as the figures neared.

"So much for covertly sneaking into the castle," Celen said, pulling back the hood of his cloak.

"I don't think there's anyone here regardless." Alluin turned his attention to Saida. "Words cannot express how glad I am to see you. Egrin has Elmerah. We're trying to find her, but it doesn't seem like there's anyone here."

She knew it. She knew the voices would not lie to her. They had brought her to save Elmerah. "Many were sent to fight my army at the gates," she explained, "but it's still too quiet here, as if everyone has been sent away. Where is Rissine? Does Egrin have her too?"

Alluin glanced at Merwyn, who kept his hood pulled forward. "Rissine was taken by the High King of the Akkeri not far from here. She used him as a distraction to help the rest of us escape. I do not know what she has promised him in return."

"Only one thing he wants," Merwyn muttered.

She was surprised that the mention of the High King caused no fear within her. He seemed such a distant threat, something she would easily face when the time came. "We cannot worry about that now. We will search the grounds for Elmerah. Rissine can take care of herself."

Feeling numb and distant, like she wasn't fully within her body, she reached into her belt pouch and withdrew the compass. She stared down at it for a moment, thinking of Elmerah. The dial turned, pointing toward the castle.

"She's here," she breathed. "We need to help her."

Celen looked toward the castle. "Do we just walk right in?"

"Have you got any better ideas?" Alluin asked.

Saida had already turned to start walking. The voice coming from the circlet had sounded urgent. Whatever Egrin planned to do to Elmerah was happening now. Perhaps she was a fool to leave Malon behind, but she couldn't very well entirely abandon their army. It was not her place to join them, but perhaps it was his. Perhaps these were the roles they were meant for all along.

Alluin jogged to catch up to her side. "I hate to ask, but where is Malon?"

She kept her eyes on her compass, making sure it did not change directions. "Outside the city with our army. They will soon breach the walls."

They reached the entrance with the others following close behind.

"Alluin," she gasped, realizing something. "Your sister headed toward the city to find you."

"And she did. I had hoped she would stay with you where she would be safe," he admitted. "I suspected you would not take her offer to sneak into the city."

She was still alive then, not another death on her hands. It was a small relief. "I almost did take her up on it. I probably should have." She reached for the door, the same door she had gone through when she had been imprisoned. She tugged the handle, but it was locked.

"Stand back," she ordered.

Brosod was the only one who listened. Celen cursed at the bright flash of light as Saida obliterated the lock. The door swung inward.

She glanced at Alluin as he lowered his hand from shielding his eyes. Even though he was without magic to defeat Egrin, she was glad he was with her. They had started this together, and now they would finish it.

She checked her compass, then stepped across the threshold into the quiet hall. "This way."

She hurried down the hall with the others following close behind, not at all ignorant to the fact that she and Brosod were the only ones carrying any weapons. And if they went up to the second floor, Celen's magic would be useless.

When they found Egrin, if Elmerah was incapacitated, it would be up to Saida to face him. Malon would not be there to save her this time.

Could she best the king of demons with only one of the circlets?

They were about to find out.

Elmerah

Elmerah stood in the center of an expansive underground cavern, lit by torches mounted in iron brackets along the natural stone walls. Egrin had forced her to move near a massive cauldron made of shimmering metal. She could feel magic emanating from it, and knew it had to be of Dreilore design.

The other hint was the Dreilore lord Egrin had summoned. He had called him Orius. He stood across from her, pouring more powdered metals into the cauldron with his long, graceful fingers. One of the powders looked like ground up moonstones. The dust shimmered in the torchlight as the Dreilore emptied the remains from a canvas sack.

Egrin waited nearby, his eyes occasionally twitching upward as if listening to something only he could hear. Thera stood far off in one corner, looking like she would rather not exist.

The small jewels in Orius' long hair glittered in the firelight as he gave Egrin a nod. "It is ready."

"Good." Egrin walked toward Elmerah. "Don't you dare move," he said when she had only thought of stepping away. "If you play nicely, you may just survive this."

Her heart pounded in her ears. He still hadn't explained what they were doing, but he was a demon, it couldn't be good.

"Hold out your arm," he ordered.

She gripped both her hands behind her back. "Tell me what we're doing first."

Every instinct she had screamed for her to move away as he stepped even closer. He leaned in toward her face, coating her cheek with his hot breath. "We are bringing someone back from the dead. She perished in your realm a *very* long time ago."

She could hardly draw a full breath. It had nothing to do with Egrin's magic, and everything to do with the fear squeezing her heart. It was impossible to bring someone back from the dead, even a demon. "Who?"

"My queen. Now hold out your arm, or I will drag you over the cauldron. No one can find you here. There is no escape."

That couldn't be true. Her friends would be looking for her. Someone would find her. Someone would stop her from bringing back the *demon queen*. Ye gods, could she be as powerful as Egrin?

His hand darted toward her. His fingers dug into her arm until she cried out and her knees buckled. He was going to break the bones in her wrist.

He yanked her arm over the cauldron and pushed back her fraying sleeve, revealing bare flesh. "Cut her."

She hunched her shoulders, scrambling to her feet and pulling back against Egrin's grip. Orius drew a long slender blade from his belt. The silver metal glowed red with magic.

Impossibly strong, Egrin held her arm still over the lip of the cauldron. She reached for her magic, and the air was instantly stolen from her lungs, knocking her again to her knees. The blade bit into her skin and hot blood flowed.

Her air returned a moment later.

"You will cooperate," Egrin said, still holding her arm over the cauldron, "or I will simply force you, then kill you. I recommend you do as I say, for your own good."

She shook her head frantically. He was bluffing, he had to be. She wouldn't be alive and conscious if he could steal her magic against her will. He didn't just want her cooperation, he *needed* it.

Reading her expression, he gave her a sick smile. "You can still summon your magic with every bone broken in your body. Your choice."

Her empty stomach rebelled at his words. Bile burned the back of her throat. What if she helped him?

Could they actually resurrect a demon queen? Someone as powerful as Egrin?

If she was going to be forced to help one way or another, she may as well stay in one piece to fight them both. "What do you want me to do?" she croaked.

Ignoring her, he gestured for Thera to approach.

Hanging her head, she shuffled toward them. Elmerah tried to catch her eye, but her long blonde hair obscured her face. She reached the cauldron, pushed up one sleeve, then held out her arm.

Orius sliced open her pale skin, just as he had done with Elmerah. A line of blood formed then dripped into the cauldron. The moment her blood hit the other contents, something clicked in Elmerah's gut. The building magic within the cauldron shifted to something tangible. All she had to do was reach out a hand and she could touch it. She *wanted* to touch it.

She tore her unblinking gaze away from the swirling magics just in time to see the glitter of tears in Thera's eyes as she stepped back.

Suddenly the feel of the magic tripled, stealing her breath. She turned her attention to Orius, realizing he had added his blood to the mix.

"Thera is a moon priestess," Egrin explained. "Her blood empowers the moonstones. Orius is an ancient Dreilore lord, his blood does the same for the metals of the Akenyth Province." He knelt before her, using his fingertips to lift her chin. "But you, you keep all of your magic inside of you. Your blood binds you to the magics in the cauldron. Orius will activate the vessel, then you will combine your magic with it and give it to me. I will do the rest."

Her body trembled. There had to be some other way out. She had to buy time. "If you needed a moon priestess, why didn't you keep Saida?"

"I already had Thera. Although, had I known how troublesome the other priestess would have become, I would have killed her at the start."

"And Isara?" she pressed. "Why keep her alive?"

He stepped back, releasing her chin. "I will bring her here when the time is right. Her blood will strengthen my queen."

She couldn't take a full breath. He had kept them all alive like sheep awaiting slaughter. The only reason he hadn't destroyed them from the start was that he wanted to use them. They had been foolish to ever think him frightened of the threat they posed. "So this was your intent all along? All of these years gathering magic, you just wanted to resurrect your queen? Are you more powerful with her at your side?"

His face twitched at some hidden emotion, then smoothed back into its cold, apathetic lines. "Even demons can love, in our own way. She was taken from me, and I will have her back."

"You're mad."

"Perhaps." He glanced at Orius. "Activate the cauldron."

Orius knelt before the cauldron, running his hands

along its sides. The shimmering metal pulsed with a dizzying glow, echoing the magics within.

Her own blood within the cauldron called to her, drawing a gasp from her lips. Waves of magic crashed within her. The power was almost overwhelming. Egrin was right, her blood had connected her to it. Centuries of power lit up her veins.

"Perfect," Egrin said, "now summon your fire."

She didn't even have a choice. The immense power in the cauldron tugged her magic free. Fire danced around her, then poured into the basin. The collision stole her breath. She gritted her teeth, fighting it.

Egrin grabbed the hair at the nape of her neck, jerking her head backward. His face loomed over hers. "Release it. Just let go."

Lightning raised the hairs on her arms. It shouldn't be possible. She couldn't summon lightning without the sky. The entire cavern lit with strange lights. Egrin gave her another tug, and lightning poured out of her into the cauldron. She tried to scream, but she had no breath.

Triumphant, Egrin let her go, then stepped toward the cauldron and reached inside. His magic touched hers, and the two melded together.

It felt like she was being torn apart from the inside. She managed one painful inhale. With what might be her final breath, she screamed.

X

Alluin

A lluin stopped halfway down a long hall, turning to Saida. "Did you hear that?"

She looked up from her compass, her eyes darting around. "A scream. It sounded like it came from somewhere below us."

Brosod had dropped to the ground, pushing her ear against the stones. "I hear a voice down there, chanting old words."

Alluin rushed the rest of the way down the hall, then glanced around a small room. Finally, he looked down. There was a closed hatch. This had to be it.

The others gathered around him.

"What's our plan for going down there?" Celen asked.

"You'll need me," a voice said from behind them.

They all turned. Brosod lifted her spear, but Saida gestured for her to be calm.

Isara stood hunching forward with her hands braced on her knees, panting heavily. "I'm sorry I could not make it here sooner. I know he has Elmerah."

Daemon stood a few paces behind her, glancing over his shoulder like he was considering running. His once fine clothes were stained and torn, and his usually glossy pin-straight hair was a fluffy mess.

Isara straightened as she glared back at him. "Don't you dare. You're going to right all of your wrongs."

Daemon crossed his arms and scowled.

"While I am ecstatic you are alive," Alluin began, "we need to go."

Isara strode across the room, her eyes hesitating for a moment on Merwyn. "Yes, it is time we put an end to this madness."

Celen hefted open the hatch, revealing dizzying lights swirling in the darkness below.

Saida moved toward the opening. "I'll go first."

Alluin placed a hand on her arm. "No, I will go. You and Isara must defeat Egrin. The rest of us are expendable."

He started down the ladder before she could argue. He had no magic, but he could *feel* Elmerah below, begging for him to save her. He could not let her down.

He reached the floor of the cavern unnoticed, then stood frozen for a moment at what he saw.

Egrin stood before a massive glowing cauldron. He had one hand dipped inside, and the other held out toward what was likely once a solid wall. Now its surface was glowing white light. Within that light, a darker shadow moved. Egrin's chant drowned out the sound of Elmerah's soft weeping. She was hunched over in front of the cauldron, wisps of her fire swirling around her harmlessly. On the other side of the cauldron stood one of the Dreilore, and just behind him a Faerune elf.

Alluin moved away from the ladder as the others descended. Isara was the first to reach his side.

She gasped, then lifted her hands. The glow of the cauldron abruptly cut off, but the cavern wall still swirled with glowing light. They were too late. Whatever Egrin had hoped to accomplish had already taken place.

Alluin's blood went cold as a female figure stepped out of the light. She was stunningly beautiful, with long crimson hair and skin like fresh milk. She wore a gown of gauzy white that nearly matched her skin. She was tall, taller than Elmerah with sharp yet delicate features.

Her eyes were all for Egrin. "I knew you would find me, my love." She glided toward him.

They embraced. Elmerah had finally lifted her head. She stared right at Alluin, her eyes shining with fear in the torchlight. Using the cauldron to brace herself, she stood. Her fire increased around her.

The female who'd come out of the light pulled away from Egrin, then held one hand out toward Elmerah. Her flames abruptly died.

"Her power is the same as mine," Isara gasped.

Egrin laughed, finally noticing them. "I promised the witch I would not kill you all. My oath is binding. Leave, and you may live for now, but she stays with me."

Saida stepped forward, the circlet upon her brow glowing with moonlight. Egrin's female held out her hand, then frowned. The circlet continued to glow.

"I am weak, my love," the female said to Egrin.

My love? The words chilled Alluin's bones. Egrin had summoned another demon.

"We will fix that," Egrin assured as he stepped in front of her, his eyes on Saida. "Attack me," Egrin warned, "and my promise to Elmerah will be void. Without both of the circlets, you are no match for me. I will destroy you all."

Saida's glow brightened, surrounding her body. She took a step toward the center of the room. "You will try."

Alluin shielded his eyes as the entire cavern lit up as bright as the moon. He heard a scream, but he didn't know where it came from. All of his senses were filled with soft white light.

Elmerah

Elmerah hunched over the cauldron, leaning heavily on the cool metal. Everything was white light. Saida's power had distracted the female demon, but in that moment of blindness, the cauldron had to come back to life. Magic pulsed within, making her skin crawl with the need to connect with that pulsing power.

Her breath heaving, she tried to push upright, but her legs couldn't hold her. Egrin had stolen too much of her magic, and it felt like he had stolen a sliver of her life force too. She blinked against the light, trying to see where he was.

If Egrin used the cauldron now, he would destroy them all. She had to act first, but she innately knew all of the magics within would be too much for her. They would overwhelm her and she would burn herself alive.

But everyone else would be safe. The cauldron had enough power to destroy Egrin . . . if she could do it before he crushed her. She lifted one trembling hand from the cauldron's rim, then dunked her arm all the way up to her elbow inside. Magic shot through her, and her own power answered. It was still there. Egrin had not entirely burnt her out.

"I don't think so," Egrin growled, stepping through the moonlight. He had one hand extended in Saida's direction, fighting off her magic. He lifted the other toward her.

She braced herself, but nothing happened.

Egrin flicked his hand toward her again, but nothing happened. He bared his teeth. "Isara!"

Moonlight swept over him and he screamed. Ice crackled off his skin.

Isara was neutralizing his magic. She knew this opportunity would not last long. The demon queen stepped into view. She held a hand out toward Elmerah.

No. She wouldn't let the demon stop her. She cast away any thoughts of her own survival, pulled in all of the power from the cauldron, then she exploded.

CHAPTER SIXTEEN

Elmerah

E lmerah woke to muffled weeping. Her entire body
ached, but she was somehow alive. The magic had
not consumed her. She sat up, realizing it wasn't the
sound that was muffled, it was her hearing. The explosion of magic had knocked her unconscious. The moonlight was gone, as was her fire. The torches had been
extinguished, but the glowing white portal remained,
granting her enough light to see by.

She staggered to her feet, stifling a cry at the sight of
her friends splayed all around. They had to be unconscious, not dead. Her magic wouldn't have hurt them.
She would not have hurt them. She had to trust it. She
didn't see Alluin, but the far expanses of the cavern were

bathed in darkness. If he was still alive, she needed to ensure he remained that way.

She searched for the source of the weeping, noticing someone crouched on the other side of the cauldron, which was now just a mess of twisted metal. Broad shoulders, clad in black, shook with heavy sobs.

Hardly believing her eyes, she staggered toward Egrin's back.

He looked at her over his shoulder, tears in his eyes. In his arms he clutched his queen. A twisted scrap of the cauldron had pierced her heart, staining her white dress crimson.

"Nothing kills like Dreilore metal," he rasped.

She reached for her magic, but there was nothing left. She had used everything inside of her, and all that was in the cauldron.

Egrin set his queen gently upon the ground, then stood to face Elmerah. "I have worked for *centuries* to bring her back. I have conquered endless cities. I have gathered magic from every corner of this land, just to see her again." He took one staggering step toward her. "And *you* have taken her from me."

She lifted her hands, reaching for her magic again, but nothing came. She stumbled backwards, tripping over the ruined cauldron. Pain shot through her as her back hit hard stone.

Egrin stepped over the cauldron, stalking her. She dare not look away to see if any of her friends had awakened. She scrambled backwards, trying futilely to escape her fate.

Her hands scraped across the stone and she fell flat on her back.

A few painfully slow footsteps echoed, then Egrin loomed over her, half of his face edged in the portal's white light. He sneered down at her, then lifted a hand. His magic hit her, crushing the air from her lungs. It pressed upon her body until she felt like all of her bones would snap. Blood poured from her nose, choking her. She couldn't breathe. Her head was being crushed in a vice.

She reached for her magic again, knowing it would not come. Egrin lifted his other hand and the pressure doubled. A crack echoed through her mind. She lost all sensation to the lower half of her body. The parts she could still feel were nothing but pain. Her face was wet with hot blood.

Her vision blurred, but she thought she saw someone creeping up behind Egrin. *Alluin.* He was alive. She was going to die here, but at least he was still alive. He staggered toward Egrin's back, hefting a spear of twisted metal from the cauldron.

Egrin lifted one hand higher, then slammed it into a fist.

Everything went black.

Alluin

Alluin shoved the spear of metal through Egrin's back, lifting his feet off the ground with the impact. He ripped the weapon free, and Egrin's body fell. The demon emperor rolled over. He stared up at his death—nothing but a harmless elf. The Valeroot elves had been the easiest to conquer. No magic, no army, no one to protect them. He had obliterated them with barely a thought.

Alluin raised the twisted scrap of metal in his hands, then stabbed it downward, piercing Egrin's heart. He had underestimated what a single elf could do when he cared about his friends and people more than anything else.

Alluin wrenched the spear free, and the demon emperor died.

He stared down at him in shock for a heartbeat, unable to believe he was actually dead. Then he tossed his weapon aside, staggering toward Elmerah. He had heard horrible cracks coming from her body. Egrin's magic had crushed her like a falling boulder.

He fell to his knees beside her, trying to figure out where he could touch her without causing further damage. He gently placed his fingertips against her throat, searching for a pulse.

Saida stumbled to Elmerah's other side, then fell to

her knees, mirroring Alluin. Behind her stood Killian, Celen, Brosod, and Isara. He didn't see Daemon or Merwyn.

Tears stung his eyes as he peered across Elmerah at Saida, mirroring him on her other side. She was the only one who truly understood this loss.

Her lip trembled, then she shook her head. "No, it does not end like this." She closed her eyes, then laid her hands gently on Elmerah's chest. The circlet upon her brow began to glow. Tears slipped down Saida's dirty face, and the circlet shone brighter.

Alluin clutched Elmerah's limp hand, praying to whatever god would listen. She had sacrificed so much to protect them all. She didn't deserve to sacrifice her life too.

He didn't deserve to lose her.

The glow from Saida's hands transferred to Elmerah, lighting her up like a star. The blood seeping from her nose slowed.

Alluin blinked. He couldn't let himself hope, but— "Please," he muttered. "Please live."

Nothing happened. Her chest did not fill with breath. Her heart did not beat. He vaguely noticed Celen and Isara both crying. Killian hung his head, muttering a prayer under his breath. Elmerah had given her life to protect them all.

The glow around her body brightened, then went out. Alluin's will to survive went with it. He gripped Elmerah's cold hand and hung his head.

"Alluin," Saida said, "look."

Elmerah's eyes had fluttered open. Suddenly she gasped, then bolted upright. Her hand tore free from Alluin's and went to her throat. She clutched at her neck, her hands flapping like the wings of a frantic bird.

He lunged toward her and gripped one hand as she managed another ragged inhale. The next breath came easier, then the next, until she was hunched forward, panting.

He lightly moved his hand to her shoulder, frightened she might collapse. Saida rocked back on her heels, her face shining with sweat, her eyes hooded. The others watched on silently as Elmerah relearned to breathe.

"Is he dead?" she rasped. "Is Egrin dead?"

Alluin moved closer to her back, carefully putting his arms around her. "He's dead. You're safe."

Elmerah leaned back against him, breathing more easily. She was bloody and beaten, but she was alive. She reached one trembling hand back to him, lacing her fingers with his and pulling him closer. "You were the last thing I saw, and if I had to die, I was glad you were alive."

He held her tight, forgetting everyone else in the cavern. "I much prefer *both* of us being alive, if you don't mind."

"I'm alive too," Celen said from somewhere behind them, his voice thick with tears, "if anybody cares."

Isara laughed, though it was more just an abrupt bark of sound. "Can we please get out of here now?"

A deep rumbling echoed her words. The cavern trembled.

"Everyone out!" Celen ordered.

Alluin helped Elmerah to her feet. Daemon was already by the ladder, ready to escape, though he did at least have the sense to let his sister climb up first.

Celen went next, carrying the Faerune elf who had been near the cauldron. She was either unconscious, or dead—there was no time to check now. Killian and Brosod went up after Celen, then Merwyn, his face hidden in his cloak.

Reaching the ladder with Elmerah and Saida, Alluin stepped back. "You both go up first."

Elmerah paused, glancing back toward Egrin's body. "You're sure he's dead?"

He nodded hurriedly. "Up you go. We're not entirely safe yet."

"Wait," Saida interrupted. Her eyes were on a nearby body.

Alluin followed her gaze as the Dreilore lord struggled to sit up.

Despite the trembling cavern, Saida stepped toward him. "What is your name?" she demanded.

"Orius," the Dreilore groaned. "I am the commander of my people. Get me out of here, and you will have a great army. Now that Egrin is dead, I can grant you anything you please."

Saida was quiet for a heartbeat as she stared down at

him. "Lord Orius," she said finally, "you killed my mother."

Alluin was anxious to escape, but hearing Saida's words, he froze.

"When Egrin died," she continued. "You lost the magic he granted you. Was it worth the cost?"

"I can grant you *anything*," Orius repeated.

Saida turned her back on him. "I already have everything I need." She walked away from him, then climbed up the ladder, calling back, "Are you two coming?"

Elmerah took one last look at Egrin's crumpled body, then climbed the ladder as the first small chunks of stone rained down from the ceiling. Orius tried to climb to his feet, but one leg was badly broken and he soon slumped back down

Alluin took one last look at him, wondering how many elves had fallen by his blade.

"Help me," he pleaded, dragging himself across the stones with his hands.

Larger chunks of rock pelleted down around him. Alluin turned away from the Dreilore, leaving him to his fate. He quickly scaled the ladder, his attention fully on the light above. Even though Egrin was dead, their troubles were not over. A battle was still taking place within the city, and only the fates knew who would prevail.

CHAPTER SEVENTEEN

Elmerah

E lmerah braced her hands on her knees in the courtyard, gulping deep breaths of fresh air. He was dead. He was really dead. There was no one left to hunt her. Her body ached, and the memory of Egrin breaking her bones was still too fresh, but she was alive.

Alluin stood beside her, watching her like she might fall over at any moment. How did he look so steady? He was always steady, even when she was about to fall apart.

She straightened, pressing her palms against her thighs to keep her hands from trembling. They were not entirely safe yet. She watched as Celen gently laid Thera on the ground.

He looked over his shoulder at her. Grime smudged

his face, mingling with his scars. He had come here with nothing to gain. He had risked his life for her. They all had. Misreading her expression, he stood and stepped away from Thera. "I wasn't sure if she was a friend or an enemy . . . "

Elmerah nodded, looking down at the elf. She had proven herself mostly an enemy, but . . . "I don't think she ever had much choice in her actions. She and Rissine were once friends."

Saida stood near Thera with Brosod. "She was the one who kidnapped me and delivered me to Egrin."

Celen looked to Saida. "If Saredoth gets to live, I'd say the elf does too."

At the mention of his surname, Daemon stepped behind his sister. Isara had lost her spectacles in the explosion, and now squinted at Elmerah.

Elmerah glared at Daemon, but her words were for Isara. "Egrin was going to sacrifice you to empower his queen. You share the same magic, perhaps even the same bloodline. Your *brother* would have let him kill you."

Isara went utterly still. After a long, tense, moment, she asked, "Is this true, Daemon?"

Daemon blinked at Elmerah, stunned. "He never—"

Isara kept her back to her brother. She had closed her eyes, fighting the tears glistening in her lashes. "What exactly did he ask you to do while we were on that island?"

"He just wanted me to bond with you. I thought he

wanted to use your magic against the witches. I never would have let him kill you."

Isara finally opened her eyes. "You wouldn't have had a choice." Her mouth pressed into a hard line for a moment, then she said to Elmerah, "I would leave this decision to you. You are the one who technically died for all of us. The fate of the elf, and my brother, are both in your hands."

Elmerah remembered her promise to Isara, that no matter what, she wouldn't kill Daemon. Even with all of the wrongs he had committed, it would destroy something inside her friend to lose her brother. She did not have to think long on her decision. "Let him live. Let them both live. I have seen enough death to last a lifetime."

Isara bowed her head. Daemon reached a hand toward her shoulder, then let it fall.

Elmerah turned toward Saida at her side. "We must put an end to the fighting. Egrin is dead. The task is finished." *Everyone he had harmed, including her mother* —both *of their mothers—had been avenged.*

Saida took her hand and gave it a squeeze. "I agree. I have had enough of death."

Merwyn stood beside her, shrouded in his cloak. There was something off about him. He stood a little straighter. If she didn't already know it was him beneath the cloak, she wouldn't have guessed it.

She had the sudden urge to pull back his hood. "What do you think your High King is doing with my sister?"

His shoulders stiffened, but he didn't reply. He took a step back and held up his hands as the others turned toward him.

Saida gasped, the first to notice that his mottled, pallid skin was now a healthy tone. She moved toward him. "Merwyn, remove your hood."

He shook his head, taking another step back. Without speaking a single word, he held everyone's full attention. Elmerah thought she glimpsed healthy flesh within the deep shadows of his hood.

"Please," Saida said. "Time is short and I would see that you are well before we move on."

His shoulders slumped, but he lifted his hands and pulled back his hood.

Everyone gasped. He was still mostly bald, but his skin was smooth, his features more neatly aligned. His pointed ears now looked just like Saida's.

Alluin shook his head in disbelief. "Hotrath was telling the truth. The Akkeri really were cursed."

"But how is he well now?" Celen asked.

Merwyn hung his head. "I stood within the light of Cindra. I believe the curse originated with the circlet. That is why Hotrath had it hidden away. He is very old. As far as any can remember, he has always been our king."

Saida tilted her head as her eyes went distant. Almost as if she could hear something that no one else could. After a moment, she blinked, and the foggy look in her eyes cleared. "We will speak more on this later," she said to Merwyn. "My army approaches."

Elmerah straightened, listening for whatever Saida had heard. She could hear the sounds of battle in the distance. But if the army of Makali was near, the sound came from a different battle taking place. Perhaps one that involved her sister.

Thera groaned, then opened her eyes. "Where am I? What happened with the cauldron?"

"Bring her," Saida ordered, ignoring Thera's questions. "I need to find Malon." She pulled out her compass, looked down at it for a moment, then started walking toward the front of the keep.

Elmerah raised a brow at her departure. "She's changed. Malon has changed her."

Alluin patted her shoulder. "I don't think he was the one who changed her. I think she figured it out herself."

"Can someone please tell me what's going on?" Thera asked, sitting up and rubbing her head.

Celen knelt down and helped her to her feet, then started walking after Saida. "Time for that later."

Elmerah managed a weak smile for Alluin, then turned and followed. She needed to find her sister. The footsteps of the others sounded behind her.

She could still hear rumbling in the castle, and wondered if the entire thing would collapse. It shouldn't. The underground cavern might take a portion of the floor above with it, but the rest of the castle should be fine.

Thinking of the poor soul who would have to live in the keep knowing that two demons were buried underneath, she glanced at Isara.

Isara was already watching her. Catching Elmerah's glance, she moved closer to walk at her side. Her hair puffed up around her scrunched face. She looked strange without her spectacles. "Thank you, for sparing my brother."

"We both have terrible siblings. Don't worry about it."

Isara smiled. "I'm not sure when the right moment will come to say I'm sorry, I almost arrived too late."

Elmerah bristled at her apology. It was undeserved. "We thought you were gone. We searched the entire island for you. I never would have left you behind had I known you were still alive."

"I know, though *someone*," she glared at her brother, "tried to convince me otherwise."

Elmerah was sure Daemon still deserved to die, but she would not be the one to choose his punishment. Isara could figure out what to do with him once she was empress—if the people of Galterra would accept her as such. She was no true relation of Egrin, but few would ever know the truth.

"We should put all of that behind us now," she decided. "It's time to move forward." *To move forward from all old grudges, including her own.*

Her thoughts moved to Rissine and she quickly shifted them away. She had made a deal with Hotrath, she must still be alive. He wouldn't have killed her until he got what he wanted. Would he?

"We'll find her," Alluin said from her other side, reading her expression. "I'm sure she's well. She's a survivor."

She nodded. "So is Vessa. We will locate them both soon enough."

She turned her attention forward, then stopped dead in her tracks. Ahead, just outside the castle gates, stood an entire army of Makali, interspersed with elves. Saida had not exaggerated their numbers. To make it all the way to the keep, they must have lost many, yet she still could not see beyond the rows of warriors. Or perhaps their losses were few, because Malon stood at their head, the Crown of Arcale on his brow. How many had he killed to reach this place?

She realized everyone else had stopped walking around her, except for Saida and Brosod, who reached the gates ahead, now being opened by the Makali warriors.

Elmerah hurried to catch up, nearing Saida just as Malon was explaining that the Akkeri had taken the docks.

He gave Elmerah a knowing look. "Some saw lightning near the sea." He needn't say more, Rissine was with the Akkeri, and she was free to use her magic. He'd been correct in his assumption that she had made a deal with them.

Elmerah looked Malon up and down. "You seem

rather unscathed for having fought your way through the city."

And he did. There wasn't a speck of dirt on him, though flakes of ash clung to his hair and dusted his shoulders. "I cannot say the same for you. You look awful. I suppose defeating a demon proved the more difficult task."

So Saida had caught him up. It surely was the first thing she'd said to him. Elmerah glanced back at Alluin and the others. "I must go to the docks. Who is coming?"

Saida stepped away from Malon. "I'm coming." She gave him a look before he could argue. "I understand now why things felt so wrong to me. Cindra was a healer, she made the plants grow. That is my gift as well. You had . . . another purpose."

He inclined his chin. "Be that as it may, I will accompany you. Just in case you are in need of . . . other purposes."

"Just say you're coming to kill any Akkeri who try to take her," Elmerah cut in, impatient to find her sister.

Malon gestured for Brosod, who edged in toward him. "Speak with the clan leaders, have them take the keep." As Brosod retreated, he turned his silver eyes back to Elmerah. She really didn't like the way he looked at her. "Shall we?"

"You let me handle my sister."

"Of course."

Isara cleared her throat. "Daemon and I will remain

here. I know Egrin is gone, but I'm worried about the portal he opened."

Elmerah tensed. She hadn't thought about that. She'd been more concerned with miraculously escaping with her life. "But it's buried. Shouldn't it be safe?"

Isara reached for her face like she might push up her spectacles, but found them missing. "Just in case, I would like to be around if anything else comes through." She gazed out across the army of Makali. "I am assuming they will help destroy any threats?"

Elmerah only then realized that Isara had been lost before Saida and Malon found them. She knew nothing of the Makali army and yet, she hardly reacted at the sight of them. Perhaps Saida was not the only one who'd grown hard over time.

Malon gestured for Brosod, who was returning from within the crowd of warriors. He introduced her to Isara. "Brosod can translate any requests you might have," he explained.

Isara nodded, taking it all in stride, then turned to Thera. "You will come with me. I assume you know the keep well? I find the idea of trusting my brother's further advice . . . unappealing."

It seemed to take Thera a moment to register that she was being spoken to, then she quickly nodded. "I am at your disposal."

Isara waved to Elmerah and the others as she turned back toward the keep with her brother and Thera scurrying quietly after her.

"She'll make a good empress," Malon said once she was gone.

Saida glanced sideways at him. "I thought you didn't care who ruled the Capital."

"No, but you do." He held out his arm to her. "Shall we?"

They moved aside for the Makali to begin marching through the gates, then started toward the docks. While Elmerah was impatient to reach her sister, she was also reluctant. She had a feeling she knew what Rissine had promised Hotrath. She would need to protect Saida, but in doing so, would she sacrifice her own sister?

She didn't know, but Alluin was with her, and Celen and Killian. Not to mention Saida herself. Perhaps she was no longer in need of protection. Perhaps when it came to friends, the whole point wasn't to simply have the strong look after the weak. The point was to look after each other.

Alluin

The city was eerily quiet, save the occasional sound of crying, or whispers from those hiding in their homes. Alluin stayed close to Elmerah, scanning the empty streets for his sister, but he was finding it difficult to concentrate. Malon had conquered the capital of the Empire in a single day. Such power should not be possessed by any one man.

He watched Malon out of the corner of his eye, walking near Saida. Could they trust the elf to not turn the power of the circlets against them? He knew with disturbing surety the answer was no. Malon would need to be parted from the circlet before any could rest easy. Beyond that, the relic should be destroyed.

He scented smoke on the wind, and heard crying as they passed another home. The circlet should be destroyed, but what if the Dreilore returned? They had fled, abandoning the city, but there was no guarantee they would not regroup and attack. And Egrin's death did not eliminate the demons coming through portals across the land. The fight was far from over, could they in good conscience destroy their best weapon?

His eyes caught movement down the hill ahead— someone peeking out of an alleyway. Another head quickly emerged, then withdrew, then Vessa ran out of the alley where she'd been hiding. She hurried up the hill with the other elves following behind her, then propelled herself straight toward Alluin. "We heard what sounded like an explosion toward the castle. We were just coming to save you!"

Alluin embraced his sister as she reached him, lifting her feet off the ground as he spun her in a circle. It was a gesture remembered only from childhood—he couldn't recall the last time he had hugged her in earnest, and he found himself reluctant to let her go.

Then Vail reached him with her judgmental air and the moment was over. He lightly set his sister on her feet. "Have you been near the port?" he asked.

Vessa shook her head, glancing at the other elves. "No, we made for the main gates, but the army had already passed." She shivered. "The destruction there— the corpses were all burned." She glanced at Elmerah, then turned back to search his face. "Is it over?"

"Almost," he assured her. "I'll explain later. We believe Rissine is at the docks with the Akkeri. We are headed that way, but you should go to the keep. Isara is there."

Vessa's eyes widened, and he realized he had left out the most important part.

"Egrin Dinoba is dead. Our lost people can rest easy."

Vail shook her head in disbelief, her eyes landing first on Saida and Malon, then on Elmerah. "How? How did you manage to defeat him?"

"It was Alluin," Elmerah explained, stepping close to him.

Feeling his cheeks burning, he quickly averted his gaze. "It was all of us. We did it together. And moving forward, we must all work toward the same goals. Humans, elves, and Arthali. We are stronger this way."

"In that case," Vessa cut in, "we will accompany you to the docks. We didn't encounter many militia on our way here, but there are people hiding in their homes, and some still running in the streets. We may very well run into trouble along the way."

He looked to Elmerah to find her giving him a small smile. He knew just what she was thinking. There may be troubles ahead, but nothing could compare to what they had already faced.

Rissine

R issine leaned heavily on Zirin as she wiped the sweat from her brow. Taking the port had almost been too easy, and she knew something else must be going on in another part of the city. The soldiers and Dreilore who fought them were now either dead, or had fled deeper into the city. There should have been more of a fight.

"We should tend your wound," Zirin said.

He had come out of the battle unscathed, which she supposed was fair enough since he was still nursing an arrow wound in his leg.

She would have preferred something like that to having her side sliced open by a Dreilore blade. She pressed one hand across her ribs, trying to slow the bleeding. "We can tend it after we find Elmerah."

"You're in no condition to fight a demon."

Some of the Akkeri milling about the port awaiting orders glanced over at his words. Perhaps more of them spoke the common tongue than she realized.

Anxious to be away from the Akkeri and closer to her sister, she nudged Zirin to start walking, then froze as a meaty palm clamped around her shoulder, sending a thrill of pain down her side. Wincing, she looked over her shoulder at Hotrath.

"I won't have you running off, witch. You must still fulfill your part of the bargain. The priestess is within the city, I can sense the circlet."

So Saida was here. As much as Rissine was dreading the encounter, with Saida here, maybe it meant Elmerah had already been rescued. "We won't find your priestess or my sister just standing around here. We need to move further into the city."

"Do we?" He still gripped her shoulder, but he was peering past her.

Rissine could hardly believe her eyes. Elmerah looked like she had spent several days trapped in Ilthune's dungeon, but she was alive. They were all alive. They hadn't needed her at all.

Malon and Saida came into view as they crested the rise in the street.

Hotrath's hand on her shoulder tightened. "I hope you have a plan, witch. You do not want to make an enemy of me."

If Elmerah was here, that meant she had escaped Egrin. Maybe she had even killed him. Could she kill

Hotrath too? Would she want to save her big sister from her own foolish mistake?

She spotted movement in some of the surrounding windows near the docks, frightened city folk unable to remain in hiding while such a confrontation was about to occur.

"You will need to release me if I am to get close to her," she said through gritted teeth. Alluin was near Elmerah. Celen and Killian were there too. Her sister would know everything by now.

Elmerah and the others stopped walking just before the wooden docks. She expected Elmerah to speak first, but instead she looked to Saida.

Saida and Malon stepped forward, and with a nod of encouragement from the priestess, a small, rather unattractive elf joined them. "I would address the High King!" Saida called out.

Rissine noticed the circlets that both elves wore. She knew Hotrath was afraid of the power they could wield together, just as Egrin had been.

Hotrath squeezed her shoulder so tightly her knees nearly buckled. Without Zirin keeping her upright, she would have fallen. Hotrath raised his voice, "Send the priestess alone, or I will snap the witch's neck!"

This wasn't going to work. No one would risk themselves for her, not after all she had done. She had orchestrated Saida's initial kidnapping. She had given her to the emperor knowing full well that Egrin had intended to give her to the Akkeri.

To her surprise, Saida patted Malon's shoulder, then walked forward without him. The small, ugly elf hurried after her. The Akkeri had fallen so utterly silent that Rissine could hear the elves' light footsteps echoing across the dock.

Saida walked straight toward them, stopping roughly five paces away to look up at Rissine, Hotrath, and Zirin. She seemed so tiny and defenseless compared to any of them, but the look in her pale eyes was not one of fear. The other elf huddled in his cloak just behind her, wringing his hands.

Observing Hotrath, Saida tilted her head. "You're the reason your people are cursed, aren't you?"

His fingers flexed around Rissine's shoulder, making her see stars. "You speak nonsense, priestess. Come with me, break my curse, and I will leave all of your people in peace. Refuse, and we will take the city for our own."

Saida smiled softly. The moonstones on her circlet seemed to shine with inner light. "It was the circlet. You had the Crown of Cindra, but not the Crown of Arcale. Cindra was a healer, and you tried to use her magic for destruction."

"You are but a child. You know nothing of this."

"Do not lie to me," Saida warned.

Hotrath's grip slackened. "H-how do you know all of this?"

"The circlet speaks to me. I do not know if the voice is Cindra's, maybe it is something else, but it told me the story of a seafaring elf. He led his crew in search of riches, pillaging islands and small villages along the way. In a temple, he found a circlet, hidden away. He stole it, and because he had magic in his bloodline, he was able to use it. But he used it for wrong, not what it was meant for, and so the gods cursed him and any who accompanied him."

Rissine stared at her, utterly entranced by the story. It seemed everyone else was too. She met her sister's eyes across the distance. It was clear Elmerah already knew what was being said.

"This was many centuries ago," Saida continued. "His crew had children, many generations, and eventually the old ones died off. Everyone but the wielder of the circlet grew old, but not him, never him. For the curse was a part of his blood. It kept him alive to watch the torture of his people."

Hotrath's hand fell away from her shoulder. She heard him step back. "You do not know of what you speak."

Saida moved closer, matching Hotrath step for step as he tried to escape down the dock. "You thought if someone like me used the circlet, someone whose magic it was actually meant for, that it would right the wrongs of your past. You thought I could save you, but this is not the case."

Rissine and Zirin both turned to watch as Saida cornered the High King. Such a small elf, and the massive Akkeri was trembling in her presence.

"You already know the only way to break the curse,"

Saida continued. "You could free your people, but you refuse to accept it."

Rissine watched the fear pooling in Hotrath's eye. Saida was right, he did know. If the curse was bound to him, bound to his very blood—

"Your death would break the curse," Saida finished. "Time and old age will never take you. You must be killed, and your people will be free."

The Akkeri started muttering around them. Those who spoke the common tongue must be translating for the others. Some reached for their weapons.

Saida stepped back, gesturing to the small elf still waiting quietly. She raised her voice for all to hear. "He was one of you until he was bathed in Cindra's light. Your curse can indeed be broken."

Hotrath looked desperately toward Rissine. Saida had her back to her, *trusting her.* "We had a bargain. Make good on your part."

Clinging tight to Zirin, Rissine gave him a bitter smile. "Tunisa tried to warn you. You can never trust a Shadowmarsh witch."

Some of the nearest Akkeri moved forward, closing in around their king.

Zirin helped her step further back. None of the Akkeri tried to stop them. They both kept their eyes on Saida as the Akkeri swarmed around her, then past her, surrounding their High King. She watched for a moment, then abruptly turned away. They all did.

Rissine turned her sights toward her sister, waiting

for her further from the docks. Elmerah was smiling at her. She hadn't seen such a smile from Elmerah since they were little girls, before their mother died.

Her little sister was all she saw as chaos broke out on the docks. Along with Saida and the other elf, she and Zirin broke free of it.

Though she was wounded and bleeding, once she reached Elmerah, she embraced her. "I know you must be angry with me, but I did it to save you."

Elmerah held her tightly. "Alluin told me what happened. He told me you ordered him to leave you behind so he could save me."

Surprised by her words, Rissine pulled away enough to search her sister's face.

Elmerah laughed at her expression. "I don't forgive you, far from it, but I am glad you are alive. You are important to me."

Rissine was so shocked, she didn't know what to say. "Did killing a demon emperor mess with your mind? He's dead, isn't he? Else you wouldn't be here?"

Elmerah nodded, still lightly embracing her sister. "Yes, he's dead, and perhaps it did mess with my mind. All I know is that I'm lucky to be alive, and with my friends—*and* family."

Rissine wanted to say more, but she was growing lightheaded with blood loss. She opened her mouth, but then her eyes rolled back into her head, and she promptly passed out.

CHAPTER EIGHTEEN

Elmerah

They gathered within the main hall of the keep, seated around a long table. The wounded had been tended, and the prisoners were locked away in the dungeon. A different dungeon from the one she had been locked in alone, this one larger and outside of the keep, beneath the barracks. Makali warriors had been sent to see what became of Hotrath and his Akkeri, but their ships had vanished. If Tunisa and the Arthali who'd hunted them still lived . . . it was a problem for another time.

Elmerah stretched her tense neck, hardly hearing the ongoing conversation around her. As far as she was concerned, the Akkeri could return to the docks. They could have the whole blasted city. She wanted to leave this place and never look back.

She smoothed her hands across the table in front of her, her eyes darting to the far corner of the massive chamber. Part of the floor had caved in over the cavern where Egrin had met his end. She couldn't seem to keep her eyes away from it, even as the others seated around the table discussed the coming days. She tugged her fresh cream-colored blouse where it snagged on her bandages, trying to focus on the words being said.

Messengers would be sent to Faerune. Saida and Malon would embark on a journey to the Helshone to fulfill their promise to their warriors. Word would also be sent to the Nokken of the Illuvian forest. Many of their people were innocent, though Killian's sister was nowhere to be found. She would answer for her crimes eventually. She chose to aid Egrin, but most of the Nokken were forced into their actions. They would be pardoned by the Capital, but that did not mean they would be forgiven by Faerune. Isara could make no promises as far as the elves were concerned. The Nokken had killed a third of the High Council, and *that* would surely never be forgiven. Nor would the Dreilore be pardoned. Any Dreilore who came near the city would be killed on sight.

Elmerah's gaze drifted once more to the ruined stonework above the cavern. She felt Alluin watching her. She knew she should be paying attention, but she had nothing left to give.

Finally, he nudged her shoulder, then nodded toward the other end of the table.

She followed his gaze toward Malon, who was staring toward the ruined cavern too. His expression gave her chills.

"Let's take a break," Celen said from across the table, and she realized he'd been watching Malon too.

The others around the table muttered their agreement, and began standing.

Alluin offered her his hand, helping her to her feet. She didn't like showing such weakness, but she was utterly exhausted, and her magic was yet to return.

Celen moved around the table to stand next to them, his attention still on Saida and Malon. His fresh tunic and breeches were a touch too small, but they were the largest to be found within the keep. He lowered his voice, "Let us visit Rissine. Her wound should be stitched up by now."

Elmerah nodded, her thoughts distant, her eyes once again drifting toward the cavern. Was the portal still open beneath the rubble? Was Egrin truly dead?

Alluin lightly gripped her arm and guided her from the room. Celen followed.

Together, they walked down a hall, then climbed the stone steps leading up to the next level of the keep. Rissine had commandeered one of the finest chambers, making Elmerah promise she'd come back to her once the meeting had dispersed.

Her legs heavily protested the final few steps, but she

made it up the stairs then headed toward the chamber. It was odd—willingly visiting her sister. Rissine . . . wasn't a good person. She was unyieldingly loyal, yes, at least toward Elmerah, but that did not erase the ugly things she had done. She had given Saida to the emperor. She had worked with pirates who were selling young women into slavery. She might one day be able to forgive her sister for what happened to their mother, but could she turn a blind eye to everything else?

She wasn't sure.

They reached the door, and Celen knocked.

Heavy footsteps sounded within, then the door swung inward, revealing Zirin. Rissine lay propped up on the bed, five plump burgundy pillows positioned around her. Lanterns cast soft light on either side of the bed despite the murky sunlight yet filtering in through the large window.

Thera sat near Rissine's feet, her back to Elmerah. She still wore her loose black dress, and looked utterly frail next to Rissine.

"Are we all friends again?" Elmerah asked caustically.

Rissine scowled. Light bruises lined one side of her face, courtesy of Tunisa. "Thera was just in the middle of begging my forgiveness. You interrupted a rather touching moment."

She rolled her eyes, then walked toward the bed.

She heard the door shut behind Alluin and Celen as they stepped into the room behind her, then stood against the wall near Zirin.

Elmerah looked her sister over. She had found a fresh white shirt somewhere, which now covered her injury. It had to be bad for her to be lying in bed while everyone stood around her. Not that Elmerah intended to show concern one way or another.

"We need to talk about Malon and the circlet," she said lowly.

A dark look crossed Rissine's face. "Yes, I've been told of the power he is able to wield. I know you've never trusted him."

She let the comment go, dismissing the sarcastic retorts passing through her mind. She sat on the other side of the bed, mirroring Thera. "There is more. He has demon blood, like Isara. He might not be their king, but with the circlet he could potentially be as powerful as Egrin."

"And he might not remain on our side forever," Rissine finished for her.

Alluin and Celen moved toward the bed.

"He was staring at the ruined cavern with an unsettling amount of longing," Celen explained.

Rissine's eyebrows shot up toward her hairline. "Elmerah told me about the portal. Do you think he can sense it?"

Elmerah shrugged. "He can sense demon portals. I would imagine he could feel . . . whatever that was."

They all looked to Thera, who hunched her shoulders further. "I don't know much about it, but his demon queen was dead. Truly dead. He needed an extreme

259

amount of magic to bring her back. I would be surprised if anyone else could summon the magic needed to use the portal again."

Elmerah shook her head. "He needed the magic to open it, not to use or maintain it. Even after Egrin was dead and the cauldron destroyed, it remained open."

"So then we find a way to close it," Rissine decided.

Elmerah's entire body tensed at the thought. That would mean clearing out the cavern—going back down there . . . but it would also mean finding Egrin's body. Assuring herself that he was actually gone. She knew without that proof, the nightmares would haunt her forever. She would always be jumping at shadows, wondering if one would turn out to be him.

She felt Alluin watching her as she finally nodded. "We will discuss it with Saida."

"Are you sure we shouldn't just wait until she embarks for the Helshone?" Rissine asked. "I imagine we don't want Malon anywhere near the portal, and it seems where she goes, he goes."

It was a thought, but she really wasn't sure they could close the portal without Saida. She just didn't know enough about it. Perhaps if they could locate the Fogfaun . . .

Alluin's hand alighted upon her shoulder. "We should all get some rest. The decision will be clearer in the morning."

Everyone nodded their agreement.

Alluin helped her stand, but she gestured for him to

wait just a moment more. She looked down at her sister. "Once the portal is taken care of, where do you intend to go?"

Her sister tilted her head. "I intended to ask you the same question."

She took a deep breath, trying to still the first flutter of panic. Now that Egrin was finally dead, there was something she could no longer ignore. *She had no home.* Now that she had fulfilled her purpose, she had nowhere to go.

She imagined Celen would want to return to the clan he had left behind in Faerune. That's where Saida eventually would go too. Killian would return to the Illuvian forest, now that his people were safe. Isara would remain in the Capital. Alluin—he had his people. He had his sister and Vail. They had accomplished what they set out to do . . . would he now wish to part ways?

All that remained was her sister. But she and Rissine were strangers in this land—their own people turned against them. Joining up with Celen's clan held little appeal. Being stared at like an enemy as the Capital was rebuilt held even less.

She realized everyone was watching her, waiting for her reply. "I will figure it out when the time comes."

Her sister watched her closely, but nodded. "If you try to run from me again, I will find you."

She let out a weak laugh. "Yes, I believe you."

She turned away with Alluin, ready to find a soft bed,

though she feared the nightmares that would come soon after.

Rissine's question plagued her as they walked down the hall, and Celen excused himself to *find a little sparrow*. She had just saved the Empire from demonic ruin—or she had at least played her part— and now everyone who'd depended on her would have no further use for her magic. She wouldn't be needed at all.

Elmerah had little trouble finding an unoccupied chamber near Rissine's. Most of the Makali had chosen to set up camp in the courtyard, and the keep was massive. The majority of the rooms would remain empty.

Alluin followed her into the chamber, shutting the door behind himself.

Her eyes burned as she thought of asking him the same question Rissine had to put to her. Would he return to the forests to rebuild his clan? Would he go off in search of a normal life?

She smoothed her hand across the heavy brocade coverlet. The bed frame was heavy oak, accented with two side tables and a large armoire pushed against the opposite wall. The window, its light slowly dimming as evening fell, was framed by thick emerald curtains.

Feeling nervous, she walked toward them. "Better not

let Rissine see these. She might try to make a new coat out of them."

She sensed him right behind her, then his hands lightly gripped her arms. He gently turned her around. "About Rissine's question—"

She held up her hand. "You don't have to make me feel better. I'm used to having nowhere to go."

"That's not what I meant." He smoothed his hands up and down her arms, observing her expression. "I just wanted to say . . . you can choose. I don't care where we go from here."

Her throat felt tight. "We?"

He opened his mouth, then shut it, stepping back and letting his hands fall. "I apologize, I shouldn't have assumed. You might have plans that have nothing to do with me."

"You thought we would continue on together after this?"

"I just assumed." He took another step back.

She hated the sudden hurt in his eyes, but it also told her all she needed to know. She moved toward him, closing the space between them. "You know, the entire time I was in Egrin's cage, I never once doubted that you would come for me." She took another step, putting herself close enough to sense his warmth. "When I thought I was going to die, I was simply glad you were still alive."

He searched her face, his expression wary, then he shook his head. "When Egrin took you—"

She gave him a soft smile. "I know."

"When I saw you standing before that cauldron—"

She pressed a finger to his lips. "I know." She removed her finger, then pressed her lips against his.

She had a terrible moment where she thought he would not kiss her back, then his arms clamped around her and pulled her close, deepening the kiss.

When he finally pulled back, she was left breathless, her thoughts swimming like a dizzying whirlpool. She inhaled deeply, then managed to say, "You know, when people see us together, they are going to stare."

He tightened his arms around her, pulling her close. "Elmerah, I have faced Akkeri, Dreilore, and demons for you. I can handle a few stares."

She laughed, then kissed him again. Suddenly, not having a physical home was entirely unimportant. The only home she needed was right in front of her. She felt it when he kissed her, and when they finally went to sleep in each other's arms. She didn't need to belong anywhere else. Home was right in front of her all along.

CHAPTER NINETEEN

Saida

Saida's eyes were so tired she had to hunch over the map just to make out the old borders. Candles burned along the edge of the table, and sconces lit the high walls of what was once Egrin's war room. Isara sat across from her, while Daemon had long since retired. The Makali clan leaders had gone too, while Brosod remained.

"We can extend this border here," Isara was saying, pointing to a line just north of Faerune. "Those lands are largely unused, and there should be enough lumber for future construction."

Saida rubbed her eyes and nodded. "Perhaps we can form a treaty with the Nokken to expand further east, though it will be difficult to convince the remains of the High Council after what happened."

While she looked forward to seeing her father, she dreaded the arguments she would be having with Cornaith and Immril once she returned home. They would not want Malon, the Nokken, or anyone else within what remained of Faerune. And she did not blame them. They had accepted the Arthali grudgingly, but only because the Arthali had never directly gone to war against them.

Malon's hand on her shoulder startled her. "You should rest. You can finish negotiating the new borders in the morning."

She looked up into his silver eyes reflecting the flamelight. "We have limited time, and much to do."

"And it is not your task to do all of it."

With a heavy sigh, she looked toward Isara. "I suppose he's right."

Isara pushed up her newly acquired spectacles. In her simple, cream-colored gown with her curls all askew, she looked like anything *but* an empress. The Makali would support her for now, but they could not remain forever. Could this strange girl with demon blood in her veins really rebuild an empire? Would the people accept her as their leader?

"We should all rest," Isara decided. "Tomorrow is likely to prove . . . *trying* for us all."

It was a vast understatement. Isara would need to address what remained of the people of the Capital.

Repairs would be planned, the lingering dead would be burned. Ships would be sent out to see what became of the Akkeri—they had departed, but that was all that was known. Had Hotrath been killed? Was their curse finally broken?

"Saida," Malon said, regaining her attention. He took a step back and offered his hand. He still wore his simple charcoal gray clothing, with the circlet upon his brow. He had been the only one to not end the day ragged and bloody. How many had he killed with no retribution?

She took his hand and stood, saying farewell to Isara and Brosod. Her own clothes were undamaged, though she was dying for a bath.

Malon held her fingers gently, leading her out of the war room and down the hall, stopping along the way to light a lantern instead of summoning his usual wisplight. A chamber had been assigned to her earlier, but she quickly requested she be moved to the room next to Elmerah's. If anything happened, if the portal reopened, or if Egrin wasn't really dead—

She wanted to remain near her friend.

They ascended the steps, then walked silently down another hall, the lantern casting long shadows on the stone walls. The keep was so quiet, she knew it must be late, but she had lost track of the hours. She felt ready to collapse by the time they reached her door.

Malon stepped ahead of her to open it, peering inside to make sure all was safe and clear. Once he had deemed the room acceptable, he moved inside and set the lantern on a low table.

She walked toward the bed, then turned to find him lingering, showing no plans to leave. "Surely you don't intend to watch me sleep."

Shadows seemed to dance in his eyes. "Of course not, it's just—"

The hesitation in his tone caught her off guard. He normally spoke with such authority. It made her soften her next words. "What is it?"

He glanced out toward the empty hall, then quietly shut the door and moved toward her. "It's just—" He splayed his hands wide. "You have what you wanted. Faerune is safe. A new alliance will be formed with the Capital, and now with the Makali."

His words made her heart beat a little faster. She had an idea what he was getting at, and she wished he wouldn't ask.

"I'm just wondering what you intend to do after we keep our promise to the Makali. Will you assume your mother's position on the High Council?"

There it was, the question many more would ask of her in the coming days. She would be expected to join the High Council, to sit up in the High Temple, making decisions for her people and doling out rewards and punishments where needed. Even just the thought of a life like that made her sick to her stomach. Not that it was a bad life—it was an honor—but it had never been what she wanted.

"I see you have considered it," he said, reading her expression.

She slumped down onto the bed. "It's what's expected of me."

"But?"

She buried her face in her hands, then muttered, "What of you? What do you intend to do?"

The bed shifted as he sat beside her. "When all of this began, I wanted a better life in Faerune. I wanted a home that would not cast out any it deemed unacceptable. I believe that if you take your seat on the High Council, that dream will be a reality."

She lifted her head to watch his face, noting his pained expression.

"Even so, I know I will never be welcome there. I knew as much from the start, but it seemed worth the price. To know I had brought about such change, even if I could not directly be a part of it."

"And now?"

He laughed softly. "I thought this conversation was supposed to be about you."

She wasn't sure what to say. She had no idea what she wanted, she only knew what she *didn't* want. "I don't want to join the High Council. I don't want to go back to my sheltered life. I want to see the world. I want to stay with my friends." She removed the circlet from her hair, twirling it in her hands. "But I don't know what to do with this." She held it up. "After we bring life to the desert . . . how can we go back to anything resembling the lives we lived before?"

He gently took the circlet from her, placing it upon the bed before taking one of her hands in his. "We could always remain in the Helshone for a time. I know Brosod would be happy to have you."

Oddly, the idea appealed to her. She longed to see her father, to ask his advice, but beyond that . . . a docile life behind the crystal walls felt like a prison. She was not the same girl who had first run away, only to be kidnapped by pirates.

"You should rest," Malon said softly. "We have many tasks before us, and after that," he smiled, "I'm sure things will fall into place."

He gave her hand a squeeze, then set it in her lap and stood, moving toward the door. He opened it, and she was almost able to let him go without another word, but the look in his eyes tonight had bothered her. She knew she shouldn't care, but—

"Malon?"

He turned with the door ajar.

"Even if we did go back, if you weren't welcome in Faerune, I would leave with you."

He stared at her, his face unreadable. Finally, he asked, "Why? I kidnapped you. I put you in danger."

She had the urge to look down at her lap, but forced herself to meet his eyes. She wasn't a little girl anymore, blushing at uncomfortable situations. "Because I remember the guardsman who saved me that day in the snow. You may not remember him, but I do."

He gave her a soft smile. He wasn't the person he once was, none of them were. Perhaps that was the point.

"Goodnight, Saida." He stepped into the hall and shut the door behind him.

She stared at it for a long while after he departed, then she lifted the circlet from the bed. She angled the moonstones so they caught the lantern light.

Please, Cindra, she thought. *Tell me what to do next.*

She waited in tense silence, but there was no reply.

Elmerah

Elmerah wasn't sure what woke her, but when she stepped into the hall she found her sister had risen too. The hall was dark save a hint of moonlight, but it was enough to see Rissine peering her way.

"Do you feel it?" she whispered.

She nodded. Oddly throbbing magic echoed through the halls. It set her teeth on edge.

The next door down the other direction of the hall opened, then Saida stepped out, quickly spotting them. "Something is wrong."

"What's happening?" Alluin asked just behind Elmerah, making her jump.

Rissine's eyes widened. "What are you doing in my sister's room?" But then Zirin's head poked out from her open doorway, and she quickly shut her mouth.

"It's this way," Saida interrupted. She padded barefoot down the hall. She still wore her clothing from earlier, with her hair pulled back into a long braid. Loose tendrils trailed in her wake.

Cursing under her breath, Elmerah hurried to follow, abandoning any thoughts of retrieving her boots. She wasn't about to let Saida out of her sight. Alluin and the others followed after her.

As Saida led them down the stone steps leading to the main level, Elmerah couldn't keep her hands from trembling. She already knew where they were going.

She took Alluin's hand as they reached the crumbled opening in the floor leading to the ruined cavern. Another female figure had arrived first.

Isara looked over her shoulder at them. "I sensed it. It woke me. I think someone is trying to use it."

Every instinct Elmerah possessed screamed at her to run. To turn around and be done with this place. Be done with demons and empires and everything else. "We have to go down there," her voice shook. As much as she wanted to run, if the portal was being used, they had to stop it.

Isara nodded.

No one argued. They had not come this far to turn away now.

Together, they climbed over ruined stones, making their way down toward the white light. Elmerah almost felt like she was floating, like her mind was trying to prevent her from facing her fears directly. She climbed down without hardly thinking, and suddenly she was there, within what remained of the cavern. It was only a third of what it had been before, most of the ground now buried in rubble. She didn't see Egrin's body or the remains of the cauldron—they were still buried.

Her attention drifted toward the portal lighting the cavern. Someone stood in front of that white light, moonstones glinting at his brow.

"Malon," Saida gasped, "what are you doing?" She took a step toward him, but Elmerah grabbed her arm, holding her back.

Malon slowly turned toward them. White light lined his features. "You said it yourself, Saida. How can we possibly go back to the life we knew before? How can we be content when we know there is more to be had?" He turned back toward the portal. "Aren't you curious where this leads? What it could be used for?"

Elmerah could feel Saida's trembling where she still gripped her arm. "You promised to take me to my father, and then to the Helshone."

"The High Council will have me killed, Saida. There's nothing you can do about that. The moment I am rendered powerless, they will see to my demise."

Before anyone could answer, sunlight flared through the cavern, blinding them. Saida tore free from Elmerah's grasp. She blinked the stars out of her eyes just in time to see Malon pulling Saida through the portal.

She opened her mouth to cry out her friend's name, but the words died in her throat. Malon and Saida disappeared in the white light, then the portal winked out of existence. The cavern turned pitch black.

"You have got to be kidding me," Rissine groaned. "We should have killed him while we had the chance."

Elmerah blinked in the darkness. It had all happened so quickly. "We never *had* the chance, and he knows it. He's making sure we never do. But why did he have to take her?"

"Why did he take her from the start?" Rissine's voice answered. "She makes him stronger."

A chill crept up Elmerah's spine. When Saida had met them in the hall, she didn't have the circlet. Without it, she would be powerless to escape Malon.

Alluin's hand found hers. "We'll get her back."

She couldn't think of anything to say in reply. Malon had taken Saida into an unknown realm, and she hadn't been wearing her circlet. She would be entirely dependent on him for survival.

Alluin dropped her hand and wrapped his arms around her, holding her tight. "We'll get her back," he repeated.

A comforting lie, and nothing more.

And in the more rational part of her mind, she realized something else. Malon had abandoned their army. What might the clan leaders do when they were told that he had run out on his promise?

What would become of the Capital when the only hope of restoring order had just fled through a portal?

What would she tell Ivran when he asked what happened to the daughter she had promised to return to him?

Saida

Saida's hands met with cold, smooth marble as she staggered forward. She braced herself against the pillar, letting it cool her cheek as she regained her senses, then pushed away.

Malon's light had blinded her, and she was forced to blink for several long moments before she could see her surroundings. Tall, white pillars stretched on into the distance, lit by the purple light of dusk.

"You don't have the circlet," Malon's voice sounded behind her.

She spun around to face him. Beyond him, a lush mountain range blocked the view further into the distance. She did not recognize the mountains, nor the surrounding pillars rising up from the cracked tiles beneath her bare feet. "What have you done? Where are we?"

He glanced around. "I'm not sure."

She choked back tears. "Why did you bring me here?" She clenched her hands into fists to still their trembling.

He turned back to her. "I apologize. I know I have broken your trust, but your trust is not worth dying for. Your *friends* see me as a threat, and nothing more. Despite all we have accomplished, I am still a traitor."

She took one quavering step toward him. She had been so close, so close to seeing her father. Everyone was going to be safe, including her. And now they might very well be lost forever. "I would have protected you."

"You would have tried."

"Why did you bring me here? If you wished to leave, you could have left on your own. I could have fulfilled our promise to the Makali myself."

He closed the distance between them, reaching out his hands to lightly grip her arms. She flinched at his touch, and his expression fell. "We will get to that eventually, although it will be difficult since you left your circlet behind."

She stepped out of his reach. "*Why* did you bring me? Why are we here?"

"Egrin made a portal to bridge the space between life and death. I thought you might like to see your mother again."

Her blood went cold. "T-that's not possible. You're mad."

He shrugged. "Perhaps. But we are here now, it couldn't hurt to take a look."

"The portal closed behind us. We could be trapped here forever, just as good as dead."

She didn't notice the satchel he carried until he tugged it forward from his shoulder. He reached inside and withdrew a leather-bound book, then a small canvas sack. He extended the book toward her. "Really, I was surprised that no one thought to investigate Egrin's private study. Everything we need to know to open a new portal is in there."

She took the book with numb hands, quickly skimming the pages. It was filled from start to finish with Egrin's words. "But he needed all of the gathered magic and the cauldron to open the portal."

He bounced the canvas sack in his outstretched palm. "I gathered what remained. Along with the power of the Crown of Arcale, it should be enough."

She clutched the book to her chest. "Then prove it to me, right now. Create a portal and take us back."

He smiled. "Not yet. There's something we must do here first."

"Which is?"

He gestured toward the book in her hands. "It's all in there. Egrin Dinoba did not only hope to bring back his lost love. He wished to find the other lost relic of the gods. A third circlet. He believed it was in this realm."

"A third circlet?" she gasped.

He nodded. "The Crown of Ilthune, the goddess of the underworld."

Her mouth went dry. The Crown of Cindra granted life and healing. The Crown of Arcale granted fire and destruction. "You want to control death itself."

His smile broadened. "With the power of the two circlets, we had the strength to conquer the Empire. With a third circlet, we would be unstoppable."

"You've lost your mind."

"You said it yourself, there was no going back to the lives we lived before. And so we will create a new world. A better world."

She stared at him as he turned away and started walking. Had she been blind to his madness all along? When he didn't look back, she hurried after him. He might be mad, but he was her only hope of returning to her realm. But she'd be cursed before she'd let him control another circlet.

She would kill him herself if she must.

EPILOGUE

Elmerah sat on the edge of her bed, staring down at the circlet grasped in her hands. She had found it in Saida's room not long after Malon had pulled her through that portal. At some point the sun had risen. She wasn't sure how long she had sat there, contemplating the circlet.

A knock on the door drew her attention. It opened before she could say anything, revealing Alluin and Isara, their arms full of old books.

"We grabbed anything that might be of use," Isara explained, walking across the room to dump the books onto the bed beside Elmerah. "If there is a way to open another portal, we'll find it."

"And if there is not?" she asked numbly.

Alluin set his books on top of Isara's, then moved to sit by Elmerah's side. He took her hand. "Malon would not have gone into the portal without a means of escape."

She believed him, but that still left the question of why he went in. What he wanted in there. She was sure it was nothing good.

Alluin and Isara exchanged a meaningful look.

"What is it?" she demanded.

Alluin sighed. "We did not want to trouble you with this until you had time to recover, but we think we should search for the Fogfaun. They transported Isara and Daemon here from the island. They might be able to help us locate Saida should we fail to open another portal."

Hope stirred in her chest. "But how will we find them?"

"The Makali scouts have reported sightings of demons lurking outside the city walls. We believe more portals are opening. The Fogfaun will want to close them."

She let go of Alluin's hand, then stood. "You both can read the books, I'll go after the demons. I will find the Fogfaun."

Rissine strolled through the open doorway, followed by Zirin, Celen, and Killian. Her sister stood a little hunched from her wound, but appeared steady on her feet. "Not without us, you won't."

Elmerah looked to each of them, then down to Alluin still seated upon the bed.

He nodded at her silent question. "We'll get her back, together."

"Together," Isara agreed. "It can't be anywhere near as difficult as defeating a demon emperor."

No one said what they were truly thinking. The demon emperor had been bad, but perhaps, a power-hungry elf with the magic of the gods was worse.

For news, updates, and information, please visit:

www.saracroethle.com

The last of my regulars had finally filtered out of the Toasty Bean cafe. It was 7 PM, an hour after closing time, but no one really paid attention to the hours. I turned the key in the lock, then started walking with a stack of books clutched in one arm. My house was only four blocks away, but that wasn't out of the ordinary in Twilight Hollow, Washington. Everything was four or so blocks away.

I rounded the corner, jingling my keys in time with my low-heeled boots. I took a deep breath, reveling in the first hint of crispness that meant summer was almost over, and autumn was on its way. My curly red hair swirled around me in the breeze.

I passed the bank, and the laundromat, then headed west down Mueller Street.

"Meow!"

I stopped walking, glancing both ways. I could have

sworn I heard a cat, but I wasn't used to seeing one on this route.

When no further meows presented themselves, I started walking again, but didn't make it far before the toe of my boot caught on a crack in the sidewalk. The books I had clutched under one arm went flying, and I followed right after them, landing hard on my hands and knees. I nearly screamed at a sudden weight on my back.

Slowly, I craned my neck to look over my shoulder, feeling like I was in a horror movie.

A black cat stood atop my back. "Meow."

I glared at the creature. "Can I help you?"

She, or he, I wasn't sure, hopped down from my back and circled in front of me, sitting down near my fallen books. I was glad it was just a cat seeing my books and not one of my sisters. A natural which shouldn't need to study witchcraft, but I was pretty sure I was defunct.

The cat watched me with amber eyes. It was skinny and a bit mangy.

I pushed myself up, sitting back on my heels. "It looks like you haven't had a meal in a while. Do you want to come home with me?"

"Meow."

"I'll take that as a yes." I gathered my books, then stood and looked down at the cat. "Are you going to let me pick you up?"

"Meow."

I took that as another yes, and knelt beside the cat,

scooping it up with my free arm. The cat did not protest, and we started walking.

"You know black cats are supposed to be unlucky," I said as we continued on. "But I think that's just silly superstition. Maybe having a black cat will make me a better witch."

The cat and I both startled at the sound of a falling trashcan around the next corner. I stopped long enough to register what the sound was, then continued on, thinking little of it. That was, until I went around the corner. I saw the fallen trashcan, and beyond that a pair shoes. A pair of shoes still attached to feet, with the toes sticking up skyward.

"Meow?"

I glanced down at the cat, then over to the pair of shoes. It was getting dark. My eyes had to be playing tricks on me. Holding my breath, the cat, and my books, I crept forward. I peered over the trashcan at the owner of the shoes. Neil Howard lay sprawled on his back, dead as a door nail.

I dropped my books as I stumbled back, but managed to maintain my hold on the cat. Fortunately the creature didn't struggle, even though I was careening away like a mad woman. I glanced frantically around the street. I had heard that trashcan fall, and Neil's death was *not* a natural occurrence. I could tell that much by the knife sticking out of his chest.

Keeping my eyes trained on my surroundings, I

pulled my cell phone from my back pocket and dialed 911.

Before the woman on the other end could say her spiel, I blurted, "I need to report a murder!"

I followed her instructions and stayed on the line, and the cat stayed calmly in my arms. Eventually the sirens came, and I spotted the flashing lights. In a small town, cops responded fast. It was a perk I'd hoped to never experience.

The two uniformed officers, a man and a woman, barely looked at me and the cat as they rushed over to Neil. One checked his pulse, even though he was clearly dead. Ambulance sirens wailed in the distance.

The male officer walked toward me, while the female stayed with Neil, watching over the corpse like someone might come snatch it away.

The officer who reached me was mid-fifties, salt and pepper hair, a bit of a paunch hanging over his dark blue slacks. "I take it you're Adelaide O'Shea?" At my nod, he continued, "What were you doing when you found the body?" He noticed my books on the ground, and proceeded to stare at them.

I chewed my lip, clutching the cat like it was my favorite stuffed animal. "I was just walking home from work. I heard the trashcan fall, and came around the corner to find Neil."

His bushy brow raised. "Walking home from work with your pet cat?" His tone oozed skepticism. He looked down at my books again.

I felt my cheeks going red. Everyone knew that witchcraft wasn't real. This cop clearly thought I was a nut, walking around with my black cat and spell books. It would serve him right if I hexed him, but I'm not particularly good at hexes. I could always ask my sister, Luna, to do it. She was the queen of hexes.

The ambulance arrived, saving me from answering any further questions for the moment. Along with the ambulance came an unmarked cop car. The officer questioning me looked at the car with a scowl, which deepened as a man stepped out.

The newcomer surveyed the scene quickly, his dark eyes ending up on me. He flashed a badge as he approached. "Logan White, homicide. Did you find the body?"

I snapped my mouth shut, afraid I might start drooling. He was the definition of tall, dark, and handsome. His skin, hair, and features hinted at Native American heritage. He was around six foot, a little on the thin side but definitely in shape. Maybe a runner.

I nodded a little too quickly as the paramedics exited the ambulance and walked toward the body. Though one still checked the pulse, it was clear they knew dead when they saw it.

"Did you see anything else unusual?" the detective asked, drawing my attention back to him.

My brows knit together. "You mean other than the knife sticking out of his chest?" I shook my head. "I heard the trash cans fall before I came around the corner, but I didn't see anyone else around."

He looked me up and down, his eyes first lingering on the cat, then on my fallen books. His eyes lifted back to me. "Give the officer here your details and head home. I'll call you if I have any more questions."

The officer opened his mouth as if to argue, but one look from Detective White made him shut it.

I set the cat down so I could gather up my books. The creature twined around my ankles while I gave the officer my information. With a final look at the body, I scooped up the cat, then hurried home.

Maybe the cat was unlucky after all, but I couldn't bring myself to set it free. We both needed a nice meal and a warm bed, and things would be better in the morning.

Famous last words, or something like that.

CHAPTER TWO

My sister Luna came bursting through my front door with a convenience store bag looped over one arm, and a bottle of wine in the other hand.

I startled, nearly spilling my tea on my white sofa, though I knew Luna was coming. I had asked her for a little bit of moral support, and for some food for my new friend.

She closed the door behind her, then looked at the cat as it came up to inspect her. Though Luna is an inch shorter than my 5'6", she's all curves and has a big presence to boot. If there's anything Luna knew how to do, it was to take up the space she deserved with her deep laughter, too many hugs, and glowing confidence.

She shucked her forest green cardigan to reveal a mustard yellow tee shirt, then knelt down before the cat, tossing her thick auburn hair over her shoulder. All of the O'Shea women have red hair, but Luna's is the darkest. My gingery hue is in the middle, and our youngest sister, Callie, has strawberry blonde.

Luna pawed through her shopping bag, then pulled out a can of cat food. "I come bearing gifts, let's be friends."

"Meow!" The cat went running toward the adjoining kitchen like he knew what he was doing. At least, I was pretty sure he was a he at this point. Someone had gotten him fixed, and I am no expert on cats, but he definitely had boy cat energy.

Luna stood, chuckling to herself, then headed after the cat. She stopped in front of the couch on her way, handing me the bottle of wine. "Be a dear and open that, little sis." She continued on into the kitchen with cat food in hand.

I caught up to find her searching through my cupboard for a dish. Finding one to her liking, she dumped the cat food on it while I poured us each a glass of wine. Luna put the little plate she'd found on the floor in front of the cat, and I handed her a glass.

Wine in hand, she crossed her arms and leaned her butt against the counter. Her chocolate brown eyes looked me over. "So Neil Howard, huh? I wonder who would want to kill him."

I took a long swill of my wine, then leaned against the other counter across from her. "You seem pretty calm knowing your sister just found a murder victim. The killer could still be in the neighborhood."

She shrugged one shoulder. "We're witches, Addy, a killer wouldn't dare come for us."

I pursed my lips. What she meant was, a killer wouldn't dare come for her. Everyone in town knew that if you crossed Luna, you would have some serious bad luck. Folk whispered rumors that we were witches, though most just took it as superstition. Even so, everyone knew that you didn't step on sidewalk cracks, you didn't say Bloody Mary to your mirror at night, and you didn't mess with Luna O'Shea.

Thinking of another superstition, I looked down at my new black cat just as he licked the last remnants from his dish. "Do you think he has an owner? He seems pretty skinny."

Luna sipped her wine and watched the cat. "I'd say if he had an owner, it was a long time ago. He needs a steady diet and a good bath." Her eyes flicked up to me. "You're going to keep him, aren't you? It's bad luck to turn away a cat when it has already chosen you."

I looked down at the cat in question, now inspecting my small dining table overlooking my backyard window. "I highly doubt this creature is a witch's familiar."

She lifted her shoulder in another half-shrug. "Well you've never had a familiar, so how would you know?"

I frowned. Just another way I was defunct. Luna was good with hexes and divination, Callie was into match-making and love potions, but me? All I was good for was brewing coffee and tea that brought people a cozy happy feeling. While my magic had helped me build a successful business, it wasn't exactly useful in any other sense.

"I don't think he's my familiar," I decided. "But if I can't find his owner, if he even has one, I'll keep him. At least as long as he wants to stay."

Luna sat her empty wine glass on the counter, then stood up straight, stretching her arms over her head with a yawn. "So what are you going to name him?"

I looked down at the cat, who blinked up at me with yellow eyes. "I think I'll name him Spooky."

"Spooky? What kind of name is that for a cat?"

I smiled down at Spooky. "Well he scared me half to death when we met, and shortly after that we found a murder victim. And he's a black cat with yellow eyes. I think Spooky is pretty fitting."

Luna turned to fill herself another glass of wine. "Whatever you say, Addy." She turned back to me and drained half her glass in one swill. "Let's make some dinner. If I'm going to stay the night to keep you safe, then you better feed me."

I crossed my arms and raised my brows. "Don't you want to know anything more about the murder? Aren't you curious?"

She gave me her best secretive smile. "Sure I'm curious, but I'm going to find out eventually. After all, you're going to be the one to solve it."

I nearly dropped my glass. Luna only had visions occasionally, but they always came true.

Spooky hopped up on the counter and nuzzled my arm until I pet him. I shook my head, looking at the cat. "I take it back. You are *entirely* unlucky."

ALSO BY SARA C. ROETHLE

Lyssandra's life is a lie. As a hunter of the Helius Order, she's dedicated to slaying vampires and protecting the innocent. What no one knows is that she's also a vampire's human servant.

If her secret comes out, her own order will execute her.

When she finds Asher, she'll cut out his heart for tying her to him, even if he only did it to save her. Even if it kills her too. But when a young girl is found dead, Lyssandra's mission is derailed. In the gaping hole where the girl's heart once was, lies single red rose. Lyssandra has seen the signature before, left by the vampire who took her uncle's life.

Karpov is one of the ancients, and his death is the only one Lyssandra wants more than Asher's. Unfortunately, Karpov is also the only being—dead or undead—who holds the key to Asher's whereabouts. If Lyssandra ever wants to find him, she'll have to work with her uncle's murderer.

Asher's death could finally bring her peace, but can she accept it when it means leaving her uncle's killer alive?

TWILIGHT HOLLOW COZY MYSTERIES
(SARA CHRISTENE)

An inept witch, a cozy town, and an old dark magic.

Welcome to Twilight Hollow, WA, a small forest town with three resident witches. Adelaide O'Shea runs the Toasty Bean, imbuing her coffee and tea with warm, cozy magic. When a black cat crosses her path, she worries her new pet might be unlucky, and her suspicions are confirmed when the next thing in her path is a dead man with her phone number in his pocket.

And the cops aren't the only ones breathing down her neck over it. There's an old, dark magic in town, and it has its sights set on Addy. With the help of her two witch sisters, a handsome detective, and a charming veterinarian, can Addy solve the murder and escape the darkness? Or will she and her new spooky pet have to turn tail and run?

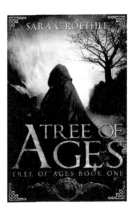

A tree's memory is long. Magic's memory is longer, and far more dangerous.

After a century spent as a tree, Finn awakens into a world she barely recognizes. Whispers of the Faie, long thought destroyed, are spreading across the countryside, bringing fears that they are returning to wreak havoc amongst the mortals once again.

Dark shapes lurk just out of sight, watching Finn's every move as she tries to regain the memories of her past. As if by fate, travelers are drawn to her side. Scholars, thieves, and Iseult, a sellsword who seems to know more about her than he's letting on.

When one of Finn's companions is taken by the Faie, she will be forced to make a choice: rescue a woman she barely knows, or leave with Iseult in search of an ancient relic that may hold the answers she so desperately seeks.

Her decision means more than she realizes, for with her return, an ancient evil has been released. In order to survive, Finn must rediscover the hidden magics she doesn't want. She must unearth her deepest roots to expose the phantoms of her past, and to face the ancient prophecy slowly tightening its noose around her neck.

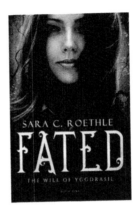

The first time Maddy accidentally killed someone, she passed it off as a freak accident. The second time, a coincidence. But when she's kidnapped and taken to an underground realm where corpses reanimate on their own, she can no longer ignore her dark gift.

The first person she recognizes in this horrifying realm is her old social worker from the foster system, Sophie, but something's not right. She hasn't aged a day. And Sophie's brother, Alaric, has fangs and moves with liquid feline grace.

A normal person would run screaming into the night, but there's something about Alaric that draws Maddy in. Together, they must search for an elusive magical charm, a remnant of the gods themselves. Maddy doesn't know if she can trust

Alaric with her life, but with the entire fate of humanity hanging in the balance, she has no choice.

FATED is Norse Mythology meets Lost Girl and the Fever Series.

The clock ticks for London...

Liliana is trapped alone in the dark. Her father is dead, and London is very far away. If only she hadn't been locked up in her room, reading a book she wasn't allowed to read, she might have been able to stop her father's killer. Now he's lying dead in the next room, and there's nothing she can do to bring him back.

Arhyen is the self-declared finest thief in London. His mission was simple. Steal a journal from Fairfax Breckinridge, the greatest alchemist of the time. He hadn't expected to find Fairfax himself, with a dagger in his back. Nor had he expected the alchemist's automaton daughter, who claims to have a soul.

Suddenly entrenched in a mystery too great to fully comprehend, Arhyen and Liliana must rely on the help of a wayward detective, and a mysterious masked man, to piece together the clues laid before them. Will they uncover the true source of Liliana's soul in time, or will London plunge into a dark age of nefarious technology, where only the scientific will survive?

Clockwork Alchemist is classified as Gaslamp Fantasy, with elements of magic within alchemy and science, based in Victorian England.

I am demon, hear me roar.

Xoe has a problem. Scratch that, she has many problems. Her best friend Lucy is romantically involved with a psychotic werewolf, her father might be a demon, and the cute new guy in her life is a vampire.

When Xoe's father shows up in town to help her develop her magic, it's too little too late. She's already started unintentionally setting things on fire, and he lost her trust a long time ago.

Everything spirals out of control as Xoe is drawn deeper into the secrets of the paranormal community. Unfortunately, her sharp tongue and quick wit won't be enough to save Lucy's life, and Xoe will have to embrace her fiery powers to burn her enemies, before her whole world goes up in flames.

Printed in Great Britain
by Amazon